Grand Army of the Republic, Dept. of New Jersey, Phil Sheridan

First Grand Gift Entertainment

of Phil Sheridan post, no 110 - Vol. 1

Grand Army of the Republic, Dept. of New Jersey, Phil Sheridan

First Grand Gift Entertainment
of Phil Sheridan post, no 110 - Vol. 1

ISBN/EAN: 9783337221027

Printed in Europe, USA, Canada, Australia, Japan

Cover: Foto ©Andreas Hilbeck / pixelio.de

More available books at **www.hansebooks.com**

FIRST

Grand Gift Entertainment

— OF —

Phil Sheridan Post, 110,

↦G. A. R. DEPT. OF N. J,↤

On which Occasion will be Produced the Five-act Comedy,

"BUNCH ❖ OF ❖ KEYS,"

At Jacobs' Grand Opera House,

Monday Evening, Nov. 11, 1889,

ADMISSION, $1.00. NO RESERVED SEATS.

Wm. A. Baker, Printer, 202-204 Market St., Newark, N. J.

COMRADE B. F. STEPHENSON,

FOUNDER OF THE G. A. R.

THE "Grand Army of the Republic" is an organization composed exclusively of those who served in the Union Army or Navy during the Rebellion; and is the outgrowth of a natural desire on the part of the participants in the conflict of arms, to strengthen and perpetuate friendships formed amidst hardships and dangers, and through the strong bonds of fraternity, enjoy the social advantages of frequent meetings of old comrades, and with them plan for the care and comfort of the sick and disabled or destitute of their number; to honor the memories of the dead, and to cherish and maintain the principles upon which the order is based. Comrade F. B. Stephenson was the originator of the first post, which was formed in Decatur, Illinois, in the Spring of 1866, and it was through his exertions that posts were organized in that and adjoining States. These lacked a central or general organization and regulations, until a meeting was held in Springfield, Illinois, in July, 1866, by the representatives of over forty posts of that State. Comrade John M. Palmer was there chosen Grand Commander-Comrade Stephenson acted as Provisional Commander-in-Chief. When posts had been formed in several States, Comrade Stephenson, in pursuance of General Order No. 13, dated Oct. 31, '66 convened their representatives for the formation of a national organization. A convention

Bryan, Taylor & Co., Publishers of the History of the Grand Army of the Republic, have our thanks for the use of the above Cut.

was held in Indianapolis, on November 20, with representatives present from posts in Illinois, Indiana, Iowa, Kansas, Kentucky, Missouri, New York, Ohio, Pennsylvania, Wisconsin and the District of Columbia.

The meeting was a large one and attracted general attention. Comrade John M. Palmer, of Illinois, presided, and the encampment adopted plans for the organization of posts, State departments, and a national encampment, substantially as they are in force to-day.

Eligibility to membership was declared in the following terms: Soldiers and Sailors of the United States, army, navy or marine corps, who served during the late rebellion, and those having been honorably discharged therefrom after such service, shall be eligible to membership in the Grand Army of the Republic. No soldier or sailor who has been convicted by court-martial or desertion or any other infamous crime shall be admitted. No person shall be eligible to membership who has at any time borne arms against the United States.

The objects to be accomplished by the organization were stated to be:

1. To preserve and strengthen those kind and fraternal feelings which have bound together the soldiers, sailors and marines who united to suppress the late rebellion.

2. To make these feelings efficient in works of kindness and material aid to those who fought with us by land or by sea for the preservation of the Union, and who now need our assistance for themselves or their families, by making provision where it is not already been made.

For the protection of such as have been disabled either by wounds, sickness, old age, or misfortune.

For the maintenance of the widows of such as have fallen, and the support care and education of their children.

3. To maintain true allegiance to the United States of America, based upon a paramount respect for and fidelity to the national constitution and laws, to be manifested by the discountenancing of whatever may tend to weaken loyalty, incite to insurrection, treason or rebellion, or in any manner impair the efficiency and permanency of our free institutions, together with a defense of universal liberty, equal rights and justice to all men.

" No officer for comrade of the Grand Army of the Republic shall in any manner use this organization for partisan purposes, and no discussion of partisan questions shall be permitted at any of its meetings, nor shall any nomination for political office be made."

Rules and regulations for the government of the order were adopted, Comrade Stephen A. Hurlbut was elected Commander-in-Chief.

The second national encampment met in the council chambers, Philadelphia, January 15, 1868; the following departments being represented in addition to those named in the first meeting: Maine, New Hampshire, Vermont, Massachusetts, Rhode Island, Connecticut, New Jersey, Maryland, Delaware, Michigan, Minnesota, Tennessee and Louisiana.

At this encampment Comrade John A. Logan was elected Commander-in-Chief. Comrade Logan directed the observance of May 30th as MEMORIAL DAY, and the national encampment, on his recommendation, incorporated the same in its organic law, making the observance of that day general and binding on the organization.

Several of the States have made this Memorial Day a legal holiday, and throughout the country its public observance attracts general attention and respect.

Comrade Logan was re-elected at the encampment held in Cincinnati, May 12, 1869, and again at Washington, May 11, 1870.

At the encampment held in Boston, May 10, 1871, Comrade Ambrose E. Burnside was elected Commander-in-Chief, and served two years with distinguished ability, doing much to place the order on a higher plane than it had before occupied.

Comrade Burnside having positively declined a third term, Comrade Chas. Devens, Jr., of Massachusetts, afterwards Attorney General of United States, was chosen his successor at New Haven, Conn., May 11, 1873. He was re-elected at the session at Harrisburg, Pa., May 12, 1874. Comrade John F. Hartranft, of Pennsylvania, was elected Commander-in-Chief at Chicago, May 12, 1875, and was re-elected at Philadelphia, June 30, 1876.

At the Providence encampment in June, 1877, Comrade John C. Robinson, of New York, was elected Commander-in-Chief. Comrade Robinson was re-elected at the encampment at Springfield, Mass., in June, 1878. The twelfth annual session was held in Albany, in June, 1879, and was a meeting of considerable interest. Comrade Wm. Earnshaw, Chap-

lain at the National Home, Dayton, Ohio, was elected Commander-in-Chief. The 13th session was held at Dayton, O., in June, 1880 Comrade Louis Wagner, of Philadelphia, was elected Commander-in-Chief. Comrade Geo. S. Merrill, of Mass., was chosen to succeed Comrade Wagner, at the fifteenth annual meeting held in Indianapolis, June, 1881. In June, 1882, the the national encampment was held in the city of Baltimore, and Comrade Paul Van Der Voort, of Nebraska, was chosen Commander-in-Chief. The seventeenth annual session was held in Denver, Col., Comrade Robert B. Beath, of Pennsylvania, was elected Commander-in-Chief. At the encampment held at Minneapolis, Minn., in July 1883, Comrade John S. Koontz, of Ohio, was elected Commander-in-Chief. The nineteenth annual session was held in Portland, Maine, June, 1885, and was largely attended. Comrade Samuel S. Burdett, of the Department of the Potomac, was elected Commander-in-Chief. The twentieth annual session of the national encampment convened in San Francisco, Cal., August 4, 1886, Comrade Lucius Fairchild, of Wisconsin was elected Commander-in-Chief. The twenty-first session was held at St. Louis, Mo., September 28, 29 and 30, 1887 and Comrade Lucius Fairchild was re-elected Commander-in-Chief. The twenty-second session was held at Columbus, Ohio, September 12, 13 and 14, 1888, Comrade John P. Rea was elected Commander-in-Chief. The twenty-third national encampment was held at Milwaukee, Wis., August 28, 29 and 30, 1889. Comrade Russell A. Alger, of Michigan, was elected Commander-in-Chief for the ensuing year.

* * *

TO MY COMRADES.

BY COMRADE S. J. SIMMONS.

Soldiers, comrades, brothers ever,
We who bore the heat together,
We who saw our ranks dissever,
 'Neath the foemen's shot and shell ;
We who on the southern plain stood,
In the dawn of our young manhood,
Loyal though scarce out of boyhood,
 Firm we met the rebel yell.

Sad those times for Jersey mothers,
Husbands, sons and stalwart brothers
Nobly died while many others
 Filled the graves we marked unknown.
Bravely grappling with their foemen,
Dying like the ancient Roman,
Fell those sons of Jersey yoemen,
 Their last thought of home.

Pale, yet firm, the Jersey soldier,
Brave of heart and broad of shoulder,
Solid as the granite boulder,
 Stood he 'mid the cannon's rattle ;
Though the dead are thickly lying,
And his wounded comrades dying,
Not a thought has he of flying,
 In the hour of battle.

Since those days long years have flown,
Comrades, we have older grown,
And the silver locks find home
 Over foreheads once so fair,
Then lets stand by one another,
Each as comrade, friend and brother,
Down life's hill we'll go together,
 Ills and joys we'll share.

But should a comrade go astray,
Though he wore the blue or gray,
Let "old Jersey's veterans", say,
 He is still our brother.
Thus we'll show the South how true,
(Though our numbers now are few,)
Are the boys who wore the blue,
 Each one to the other.

PHILIP H. SHERIDAN.

Of the heroes whose glory
History loves to name,
Whose deeds will live in story
With everlasting fame,
No braver, truer soldier
Our starry banner bore
Than gallant Philip Sheridan,
Of famous Shenandoah.

PHILIP HENRY SHERIDAN, born in Albany, N. Y., March 6, 1831. He entered the United State Military Academy, July 1, 1848, and graduated July 1, 1853. His standing was 34 in a class of 52, in which James B. McPheason was the head. General John M. Schofield and the Confederate General, John B. Hood, were also his classmates. He was appointed a Brevet Second Lieutenant in the 3d Infantry. After service in Kentucky, Texas and Oregon, he was commissioned Second Lieutenant in the 4th Infantry November, 22, 1854. Promoted to First Lieutenant March 1, 1861, and Captain in the 13th Infantry May 14, 1861. In December of the same year he was Chief Quartermaster and Commisary in Southwestern Missouri. In the Mississippi campaign from April to September, 1862, he was Quartermaster at General Halleck's headquarters. During the advance on Corinth it became manifest that his true place was in the field. May 20, 1862, he received the appointment of Colonel of the 2d Michigan Cavalry. July 1st, sent on a raid to Boonsville, Miss. He did excellent service in the pursuit of the enemy from Corinth to Baldwin, and in many skirmishes during July and at the battle of Boonville. In reward for

The above Cut was kindly furnished by Hunt & Eaton, Publishers of Ridpath's History of the United States.

his skill and courage he was made Brig.-General of Volunteers July 1st. October 1st he was placed in command of the Eleventh Division of the Army of the Ohio, in which capacity he took part in the successful battle of Perryville, on October 8th, between the armies of General Buell and General Bragg, at the close of which the latter retreated from Kentucky. In this action Sheridan was particularly distinguished. After the enemy had driven back McCook's corps and were pressing upon the exposed left flank of Gilbert, Sheridan, with General Robert B. Mitchell, arrested the tides, and, driving them back through Perryville, re-established the broken line. His force, with the army, marched to the relief of Nashville in October and November. He was then placed in command of a division in the Army of the Cumberland, and took part in the two days' battle of Stone River; or, Murphreesboro December 31, 1862, and January 3, 1863. Buell had been relieved from the command of the army on October 30th, and Rosecrans promoted in his place. The Confederate army was still under Bragg. The left of Rosecrans was strong and his right comparatively weak. So the right was simply to hold its ground while the left should cross the river. The project of Bragg, well conceived, was to crush the Union right, and he almost succeeded, as division after division was driven back, until Cheatham attacked him in front, while Clabourn assayed to turn his flank and Sheridan was reached. The fate of the day seemed to be in his hands. He resisted vigorously, then advanced and drove the enemy back, changing front to the South—a daring maneuver in battle—held the overwhelming force in check and retired only at the point of the bayonet. This brilliant feat of arms enabled Rosecrans to form a new line in harmony with his overpowered right. Sheridan said, laconically, to Rosecrans when they met on the field, pointing to the wreck of his division, which had lost 1,630 men : "There are all that are left." After two days of indecision and desultory attempts, Bragg abandoned Murphreesboro and fell back to Tullahoma, while Rosecrans waited for a rest at that place.

Sheridan's military ability had been at once recognized and acknowledged by all, and he was appointed a Major-General of Volunteers, to date from December 31, 1862. He was engaged in the pursuit of Van Dorn to Columbia and Franklin during March, and captured a train and many prisoners at Eaglesville. He was with the advance on Tullahoma from June 24th to July 4, 1863, taking part in the capture of Winchester, Tenn., June 27th. He was with the army in the crossing of the Cumberland Mountains and the Tennessee River, from August 15th to September 4th, and in the severe battle of Chickamauga September 19th and 20th. The Union right, under McCook, was driven from the field and was in imminent danger of being cut off, but General George H. Thomas held the centre with an iron grip, and General Thomas L. Crittenden commanded the left. Bragg maneuvered to turn the left and cut Rosecrans off from Chattanooga. During the battle there was a misconception of orders, which left a gap in the centre of the line which the enemy at once entered, the right being thus thrown out of the fight. The centre was greatly imperilled. For some time the battle seemed irrecoverably lost, but Thomas, since called the " Rock of Chickamauga," held firm. Sheridan, alone, rallied many soldiers of the retreating centre and joined Thomas, and in spite of the fierce and repeated attack of the enemy, the entire force fell slowly back in good order within the defences of Chattanooga, whither Crittenden and Rosecrans had gone.

Rosecrans was superseded by Thomas, to whom was presented a problem apparently incapable of solution. He was ordered to hold the place to the point of starvation, and he said he would. The enemy had posession of the approaches by land and water. Men and animals were starving, and forage and provisions had to be hauled a distance of seventy-five miles. General Grant was then invested with the command of all the armies contained in the new military Division of the Mississippi, embracing the departments of the Ohio, the Cumberland and the Tennessee. He reached Chattanooga on October 23d, and ordered the troops relieved by the capture of Vicksburg to join him, and Sherman came with his corps.

Sheridan was engaged in all the operations around Chattanooga under the immediate command and personal observations of General Grant, and played an important part in the battle of Mission Ridge. From the centre of the Union line he led the troops of his division from Orchard Knob, and, after carrying the intrenchments and rifle pits at the foot of the mountain, instead of using his discretion to pause there, he moved his division forward to the top of the ridge, and drove the enemy across the summit and down the opposite side. In this action he first attracted the marked attention of General Grant, who saw that he might be one of his most useful lieutenants in the future—a man with whom to try its difficult and delicate problems. A horse was shot from under him in this action, but he rushed on in the pursuit of Mission Mills, with other portions of the corps of Thomas harrassing the rear of

12

Going into Action.

the enemy, for Bragg, having abandoned all his positions on Look Out Mountain, Chatta-nooga Valley and Missionary Ridge, was in rapid retreat towards Dalton. After further operations connected with occupancy of East Tennessee, Sheridan was transferred by Grant to Virginia, where, April 4, 1864, he was placed in command of the cavalry corps of the Army of the Patomac, all the cavalry being consolidated to form that command. Here he seemed in his element. To the instincts and talents of a General he joined the fearless dash of a dragoon. Entering with Grant upon the overland campaign, he took part in the bloody battle of the Wilderness on the 5th and 6th of May, 1864. Constantly in the van or on the wing, he was engaged in raids threatening the Confederate flanks and rear. His fight at Todd's Tavern, on the 7th of May, was an important aid to the movement of the army. His capture of Spotsylvania Court House, on the 8th of May, added to his reputation for timely dash and daring, but more assonishing was his great raid from the 9th to the 24th of May. He cut the Virginia Central and the Richmond and Fredericksburg Railroads and made his appearance in good condition near Chatfield Station on the 25th of May. In this raid, having under him kindred spirits in Merritt, Custer, Wilson and Gregg, he first made a descent upon Beaver Dam trains and recaptured about 400 men who had been made prisoners. At Yellow Tavern, on the 11th of May, he encountered the Confederate cavalry, under J. E. B. Stuart, who was killed in the engagement. He next moved upon the outer defenses of Richmond, rebuilt Meadow's Bridge, went to Bottom Bridge, and reached Haxall's on the 14th of May. He returned by Hanovertown and Totopotomoy Creek, having done much damage, created fears and misgivings, and won great renown with little loss. He led the advance to Cold Harbor, crossing the Pamunky at Hanovertown on the 27th of May, fought the cavalry battle of Hawe's Shop on the 28th, and held Cold Harbor until General William F. Smith came up with the 6th corps to occupy the place. The bloody battle of Cold Harbor was fought on the 31st of May and 3d of June. Setting out on the 7th of June, Sheridan made a raid toward Charlotteville, where he expected to meet the Union forces under General Hunter. This movement, it was thought, would force Lee to detach his cavalry. Unexpectedly, however, Hunter made a detour to Lynchburg, and Sheridan, unable to join him, returned to Jourdan's point, on the James River. Thence, after again cutting the Virginia Central and Richmond and Fredericksburg Railroads and capturing 500 prisoners, he joined for a brief space the Army of the Potomac. In quick succession came the cavalry actions of Trevillian Station, fought between Wade Hampton and Torbert, on the 11th and 12th of June, and Tunstall Station, on the 21st of June, 1864, in which the movements were points to cover the railroad crossings of the Chickahoming and the James River. There was also a cavalry affair of a similar nature at St. Mary's Church on the 24th of June. The vigor, judgment and dash of Sheridan had now marked him in the eyes of Grant as fit for a far more important station. Early in August, 1864, he was placed in command of the Army of the Shenandoah, formed in part from the army of Hunter, who retired from the command, and from that time to the end of the war Sheridan seems to have never encountered a military problem too difficult for his solution. His new army consisted at first of the 6th corps, two divisions of the 8th, and two cavalry divisions, commanded by Generals Torbert and Wilson, which he took with him from the Army of the Potomac. Four days later (the 7th of August), the scope of his command was constituted the middle military division. He had an arduous and difficult task before him to clear the enemy out of the Valley of Virginia, break up his magazines and relieve Wash ington from chronic terror. Sheridan grasped the situation at once. He posted his forces in front of Berryville, while the enemy, under Earley, occupied the west bank of Opequan

14

Creek, and covered Winchester in his division. Besides the 6th corps, under Wright, and the 8th, under Crook, Sheridan had received the addition of the 19th, commanded by Emmory. Torbert was placed in command of all the cavalry. Having great confidence in Sheridan, Grant yet acted with a proper caution before giving him the final order to advance. He went from City Point to Harper's Ferry to meet Sheridan, and told him he must not move till Lee had withdrawn a portion of the Confederate force in the Valley. As soon as that was done he gave Sheridan the laconic direction : "Go in." He says in his report : "He was off promptly on time, and I may add that I have never since deemed it necessary to visit General Sheridan before giving him orders." On the morning of the 19th of September Sheridan attacked Earley at the Crossing of the Opequan, fought him all day, drove him through Winchester and sent him whirling up the Valley, having captured 5,000 prisoners and 5 guns. The enemy did not stop to reorganize until they reached Fiser's Hill, thirty miles south of Winchester. Here Sheridan again came up and dislodged him, driving him through Harrisonburg and Staunton, and in scattered portions through the passes of the Blue Ridge. For these successes he was made a Brig.-General in the regular army on the 10th of September. Returning leisurely to Strasburg, he posted his army for a brief repose behind Cedar Creek, while Torbert was dispatched on a raid to Staunton with orders to devastate the country, so that, should the enemy return, he could find no subsistance, and this was effectually done. To clear the way for an advance, the enemy now sent a new cavalry General, Thomos L. Rosser, down the Valley, but he was soon driven back in confusion. Earley's army being re-enforced by a portion of Longstreet's command, again moved forward with celerity and secrecy. Fording the north fork of the Shenandoah on the 18th of October, approached rapidly and unobserved, under favor of fog and darkness, to within 600 yards of Sheridan's left flank,'which was formed by Crook's corps. When, on the early morning of the 19th, they leaped upon the surprised Union forces, there was an immediate retreat and the appearance of an appalling disaster, the 8th corps was rolled up, the exposed centre in turn gave away, and soon the whole army was in retreat. Sheridan had been absent in Washington, and at this juncture had just returned to Winchester, twenty miles from the field. Hearing the sound of battle, he rode rapidly and arrived on the field at 10 o'clock. As he rode up he shouted to the retreating troops : "Face the other way, boys ; we are going back." Many of the Confederates had left their ranks to plunder, and the attack was made upon their disorganized battalions, and was successful. A portion of their army, ignorant of the swiftly coming danger, was intact, and had determined to give a finishing blow to the disorganized Union forces. This was met and hurled back in two columns with cavalry supports. The enemy's left was soon routed, the rest followed, never to return, and the Valley was thus finally rendered impossible for occupancy by Confederate troops. They did not stop until they had reached Staunton, and pursuit was made as far as Mount Jackson. They had lost in the campaign 16,952 killed or wounded and 13,000 prisoners. Under orders from Grant, Sheridan devastated the Valley. He has been censured for this, as if it were wanton destruction and cruelty. He destroyed the barns and the crops, mills, factories, farming utensils, etc., etc., and drove off all the cattle, sheep and horses, but, as in similar cases in European history, although there must have been much suffering and some uncalled for rigor, this was necessary to destroy the resources of the enemy in the Valley, by means of which they could continually menace Washington and Pennsylvania.

The terms of the President's order making Sheridan a Major-General in the regular army were : "For personal gallantry, military skill and just confidence in the courage and patriotism of his troops, displayed by Philip H. Sheridan on the 19th day of October, at Cedar Run, where, under the blessing of Providence, his routed army was reorganized, a great nation's disaster averted, and a brilliant victory achieved over the rebels for the third time in pitched battle within thirty days, Philip H. Sheridan is appointed Major-General in the Regular Army of the United States, to rank as such from the 8th day of November, 1864." The immediate tribute of Grant was equally strong, in a general order that each of the armies under his command should fire a salute of 100 guns in honor of these victories. He says of the last battle, "That it stamps Sheridan what I have always thought him, one of the ablest of generals." On the 9th of February, 1865, Sheridan received the thanks of Congress for the gallantry, military skill and courage displayed in the brilliant series of victories achieved by his army in the Valley of the Shenandoah, especially at Cedar Run. During the remainder of the war Sheridan fought under the direct command of Grant, and always with unabated vigor and consummate skill. In the days between February 27th and March

24th, 1865, he conducted, with 10,000 cavalry, a colossal raid from Winchester to Petersburg, destroying the James River and Kanawha Canal, and cutting the Gordonsville and Lynchburg, the Virginia Central and the Richmond and Fredericksburg R. R. during this movement. On March 1st he secured the bridge of the middle fork of the Shenandoah, and on the 2d he again routed Earley at Waynesboro, pursuing him towards Charlottsville. He joined the Army of the Potomac and shared in all its battles. From Grant's General Orders, to Meade, Orde and Sheridan, on March 24th, 1865, we learn that a portion of the army was to be moved along its left to turn the enemy out of Petersburg ; that the rest of the army was to be ready to repel and take advantage of attacks in front, while General Sheridan, with his Cavalry, should go out to destroy the South Side and Danville Railroads, and take measures to intercept the enemy should he evacuate the defences of Richmond. On the morning of the 29th of March the movement began. Two corps of the Army of the Potomac were moved towards Dinwiddie Court House, which was, in a measure, the key of the position to be cleared by Sheridan's troops. The Court House lies in the fork of the South Side and Weldon Railroad, which met in Petersburg. A severe action took place at Dinwiddie, after which Sheridan advanced to Five Forks on the 31st of March. He was strongly opposed by the bulk of Lee's column, but, dismounting his cavalry and deploying, he checked the enemy's progress, retiring slowly upon Dinwiddie. Of this movement General Grant says : "Here he displayed great generalship, instead of retreating with his whole command, to tell the story of superior forces encountered, he deployed his cavalry on foot. He dispatched to me what had taken place, and that he was dropping back slowly on Dinwiddie." There, reinforced and assuming additional command of the 5th corps, 12,000 strong, he returned on April 1st with it and 9,000 cavalry to Five Forks and ordered General Merit to make a point of turning the enemy's right, while the 5th corps struck their left flank. The Confederates were driven from their strong line and routed, fleeing westward, leaving 6,000 prisoners in his hands. Sheridan immediately pursued. Five Forks was one of the most brilliant and decesive of the engagements of the war, and compelled Lee's evacuation of Petersburg and Richmond. Sheridan was engaged at Sailors Creek on the 6th of April, where he captured sixteen guns, and pursuing the Army of Northern Virginia, and aiding largely to compel the final surrender. He was present at the surrender of Appomattox Court House on the 9th of April. He made a raid to South Boston, North Carolina, on the River Dan, on the 24th of April, returning to Petersburg on the 3d of May, 1865.

After the war Sheridan was in charge of the Military Division of the Gulf from the 17th of July to the 15th of August, 1866, which was then created the Department of the Gulf, and remained there until the 11th of March, 1867. From the 12th of September to the 6th of March he was in command of the Department of Missouri, his headquarters at Fort Leavenworth, Kansas. Thence he conducted a winter campaign against the Indians, after which he took charge of the Military Division of the Mississippi, with headquarters at Chicago. When Ulysis S. Grant became President, on the 4th of March, 1869, General Wm. T. Sherman, who was General-in-Chief, and Sheridan was promoted to Lieut.-General, with the understanding that both of these titles should cease with the men holding them. In 1870 Sheridan visited Europe to witness the conduct of the Franco-Prussian war. He was with the German Staff during the battle of Gravelott, and presented some judicious criticisms of that campaign. He commanded the Western and Southwestern Military Divisions in 1878. On the retirement of General Sherman in 1883, the Lieut.-General became General-in-Chief. In recognition of his claims, a bill was passed by the unanimous consent of both Houses of Congress, and was promptly signed by President Cleveland, restoring for him, and during his

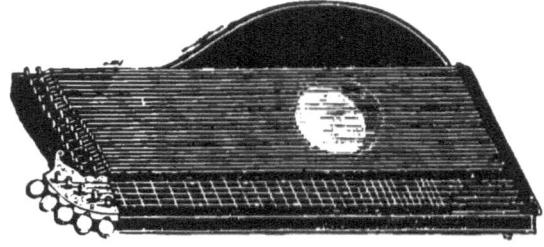
· IN

lifetime, the full rank and emolument of Lieut.-General. He was the 19th General-in-Chief of the United States Army.

Sheridan never was defeated, but frequently plucked victory from the very jaws of defeat. He was thoroughly trusted and admired, and loved by his officers and men. He bore the nick-name of Little Phil, a term of endearment due to his size. He was below the middle height, but powerfully built, with a strong cast of countenance, indicative of valor and resolution. He was trustful to a remarkable degree, modest and reticent. He was a model soldier and general, a good citizen in all the relation of public and private life, thoroughly deserving the esteem and admiration of all who knew him.

In 1879 Sheridan married Miss Rucker, the daughter of General Daniel H. Rucker, of the United States Army. During a western journey in connection with the duties of his position, he was stricken down with sickness which terminated in death on August 5, 1888, at Nonquitt, Mass. In religion he was a Roman Catholic, and devoted to his duties as such. He was the author of "Personal Memoirs," 2 vols., New York, 1888.

SHERIDAN'S RIDE.

BY T. B. READ.

Up from the South at break of day,
Bringing from Winchester fresh dismay.
  The affrighted air with a shudder bore,
  Like a herald in haste, to the chieftain's door,
  The terrible grumble, and rumble, and roar,
  Telling the battle was on once more,
And Sheridan twenty miles away.

And wider still those billows of war
Thundered along the horizon's bar ;
And louder yet into Winchester rolled
The roar of that red sea uncontrolled.
Making the blood of the listener cold,
As he thought of the stake in that fiery fray,
And Sheridan twenty miles away.

But there is a road from Winchester town,
A good broad highway leading down ;
And there, through the flush of the morning light,
A steed as black as the steeds of night
Was seen to pass, as with eagle flight.
As if he knew the terrible need ;
He stretched away with his utmost speed ;
Hills rose and fell ; but his heart was gay,
With Sheridan fifteen miles away.

Still sprung from those swift hoofs, thundering
    South,
The dust, like smoke from the cannon's mouth ;
Or the trail of a comet, sweeping faster and faster,
Foreboding to traitors the doom of disaster.
The heart of the steed and the heart of the master
Were beating like prisoners assaulting their walls,
Impatient to be where the battle-field calls ;
Every nerve of the charger was strained to full
    play,
With Sheridan only ten miles away.

Under his spurning feet the road
Like an arrowy Alpine river flowed,
And the landscape sped away behind
Like an ocean flying before the wind,
And the steed, like a bark fed with furnace ire,
Swept on, with his wild eye full of fire.
But lo ! he is nearing his heart's desire ;
He is snuffling the smoke of the roaring fray,
With Sheridan only five miles away.

The first that the General saw were the groups
Of stragglers, and then the retreating troops,
What was done ? what to do ? a glance told him
    both,
Then striking his spurs, with a terrible oath,
He dashed down the line, 'mid a storm of huzzas,
And the wave of retreat checked its course there,
    because
The sight of the master compelled it to pause.
With foam and with dust the black charger was
    gray :
By the flash of his eye, and the red nostril's play,
He seemed to the whole great army to say,
" I have brought you Sheridan all the way
From Winchester, down to save the day !

Hurrah ! hurrah for Sheridan !
Hurrah ! hurrah for horse and man !
And when their statues are placed on high.
Under the dome of the Union sky,
The American soldiers' Temple of Fame ;
There with the glorious General's name.
Be it said, in letters both bold and bright,
  " Here is the steed that saved the day.
By carrying Sheridan into the fight,
    From Winchester, twenty miles away !"

TEACHER—"John, give me a sentence containing the word 'contents.'" John—"The 'contents' of a cow is milk."

DON'T ridicule the poor man who supports ten or a dozen dogs. Perhaps that's the only way he has to keep pup.

SUNDAY-SCHOOL.—Teacher—"What must we do before we can have our wrongs forgiven ?" Bright Scholar—"We must first commit the wrongs."

"Our Flag."

By Comrade Jas. F. Lovering.

" Flag of the Seas! on ocean wave
Thy stars shall glitter o'er the brave."

" Flag of the brave! thy folds shall fly,
The sign of hope and triumph high."

OUR flag was woven on the loom of the Revolution by the indomitable valor, the unwavering determination and invincible faith of hearts that knew no fear and would endure no wrong. It was consecrated to liberty and equal rights, to the security of the citizen and the sovereignty of the people. Under its sheltering folds and in defence of the principles for which it stands, our heroic and immortal dead rallied, and fought, and fell, and were promoted. For its honor and supremacy we have toiled, and suffered, and prayed. Beneath its radiant folds no miscreant fraud, no treachery with assassin heart, no sullen and vindictive treason ought to live.

Its shelter should protect only industry, good faith, self-sacrificing patriotism, that an honorable past may not fail of its just deserts ; that the present may be strengthened in devotion to acknowledged duty ; that the future may realize what a loyal faith may encourage us to expect. All hail our starry flag ! See how its stars glow with celestial light ; see how its crimson throbs, as if it still felt the pulse of the brave hearts that have defended it ; see how its white symbolizes an unstained loyalty ; see how its blue still mirrors the heavens, in whose purity its stars first learned how to shine.

See how the eagle on its staff, with half-spread pinions and vigilant eyes, watches against any rattlesnake that may lurk in the grass, or any buzzard that may anywhere have fattened on carrion. Comrades, let our flag be dear to us ; let it be set high above us; let nothing be dearer ; let nothing be higher, save only the austere and sublime symbol of our faith—the cross of Jesus Christ, our Lord. Amen.

THE GRAND ARMY BADGE.

They pinned upon a veteran's breast
 A star from cannon cast.
His eyes lit up as though the badge
 Recalled the vanished past.
Old comrades gathered 'round and talked
 About a bloody war,
And all who heard their stories knew
 The meaning of the star.

It means that treason raised its head
 A few short years ago ;
It means that Sumpter's starry flag
 Went down before the foe ;
It means that to the rescue sprang
 Fresh youth and hoary sire ;
It means the charge of Donaldson
 And Shiloh's rain of fire.

It meens Antietam's bloody bridge,
 · Where hundreds fought and fell ;
It means the dash at Mission Ridge
 And Round Top's lurid hell ;
It means the heights of Fredericksburg
 And Lookout's lofty crest,
Old Chickamauga's crimson tide,
 And Pea Ridge in the West.

It means a week of fighting, with
 Virginia's burning sun;
It means the dash through Winchester.
 With Early on the run;
It means a crimson New Year's Day,
 Amid storm-riven snow;
It means a swoop with "Little Phil,"
 A charge with " Fighting Joe."

It means the death-struck Wilderness
 And Nashville's glorious day;
It means a ride with Farragut
 Thro' fire in Mobile Bay;
It means the long heroic march
 With Sherman to the sea;
It means a dash with Averill
 Around the flanks of Lee.

It means some noble work with Grant,
 When glory led the van;
It means that he who wears it is
 A true and loyal man;
It means that lonely midnight watch
 In miasmatic pen;
It means a night of horror in
 The ghastly prison pen.

It means long nights of anguish on
 The wounded's churlish cot:
It means the gloomy hospital,
 With fever raging hot;
It tells a tale of suffering, which
 The fair cannot believe;
It means, oh, my! a missing leg,
 It means an empty sleeve.

It means that comrades, good and true,
 Fell at the wearer's side;
It means that fathers, brothers, sons,
 Around him braveiy died;
It means that when they homeward turned
 From their last battle flame
In all this land, from sea to sea,
 No human wore a chain.

No wonder that his eyes lit up
 When some one spoke of war;
No wonder that he smiled upon
 His ribbon and his star.
I know he hardly saw it through
 A mist of blinding tears.
No wonder! for a prouder badge
 No living hero wears.

—24—

The Grand Army Badge is of bronze, made from cannon captured in various decisive battles during the late Rebellion. The design as here given and adopted by the Grand Army of the Republic, was arranged by Comrade F. A. Starring. In the centre of the badge is the figure of the goddess of Liberty, representing loyalty ; on either side a soldier and a sailor clasping hands, representing fraternity; and two children receiving benediction and assurance of protection from the comrades, representing Charity. On each side of the group is the national flag and the eagle, representing freedom; and the ax or bunch of rods represent our union. In each of the five points of the star is the insignia of the different arms of the service, viz.: the bugle for infantry, cross cannon for artillery, cross muskets for the marine, cross swords cavalry, and the anchor for Sailors. Over the central group are the words: "Grand Army of the Republic," and under, the word and figures, "1861—Veteran—1866," commemorating the commencement and close of the Rebellion, and also the date of the organization of the order. The reverse side represents a branch of laurel—the crown and reward of the brave—in each point of the star; the national shield in the centre, surrounded by the twenty-four recognized Corps Badges, numerically arranged, each on a keystone and all linked together showing that they are united and will guard and protect the shield of the nation. Around the centre is a circle of stars, representing the states of the Union and the departments constituting the Grand Army of the Republic. The clasp is composed of the figure of an eagle, with cross cannon and ammunition, representing defense; the eagle with drawn sword hovering over and always ready to protect from insult or dishonor the national flag, which is also the emblem and ribbon of the order.

Remember.

Remember that a gladsome smile
Is like a sunbeam gay;
It has the power to cheer the hour
And chase the clouds away.

Grand Army of the Republic,

DEPARTMENT OF NEW JERSEY.

EACH of the States of our Union have their own separate Departments, with power to make laws for the government of the various Posts organized in their respective jurisdiction. All are alike subject to the National Encampment. Comrade Edward Jardine, one of the representatives present at the Pittsburg Convention, September 24, 1866, from New Jersey, was there initiated as a member of the Grand Army of the Republic. He served as an aid-de-camp on the staff of the Commander-in-chief, and also Provisional Commander. He called a meeting to organize a Department for New Jersey, which was held in Newark on December 10, 1867. At this meeting he was elected the First Department Commander, and was re-elected at the Trenton encampment, April 9, 1868, serving with distinguished ability, doing much to advance the organization, and later, on removing to New York, became the Commander of that Department. At the Encampment held in Newark, January 24, 1869, Comrade William Ward was elected Department Commander, and re-elected at the Encampment held in Camden, January 13, 1870. At the Encampment held in Elizabeth, January 25, 1871, Comrade Richard H. Lee was elected Department Commander, and re-elected at the Encampment held in Paterson, January 29, 1872. At the Sixth Encampment, held in Trenton January 28, 1873, Comrade John R. Goble was elected Department Commander. At the Seventh Encampment, held in Newark January 21, 1874, Comrade Charles Burrows was elected Department Commander, and re-elected at the Encampment held in New Brunswick, January 28, 1875. At the Ninth Encampment, held in Trenton January 27, 1876, Comrade Edward W. Davis was elected Department Commander. At the Tenth Annual Encampment, held in Elizabeth, January 31, 1877, Comrade John Mueller was elected Department Commander, and re-elected at the Encampment held in Passaic, January 30, 1878. The Twelfth Encampment, held in Orange January 23, 1879, elected Comrade

—28—

Samuel Hufty. The Thirteenth Encampment, held in Trenton February 25, 1880, elected Comrade George W. Gile Department Commander. The Fourteenth Encampment, held in Camden February 24, 1881, elected Comrade Charles H. Houghton Department Commander. The Fifteenth Encampment, held in Trenton on January 25, 1882, elected Comrade Edward L. Campbell Department Commander. The Sixteenth Encampment, held in Trenton January 25, 1883, elected Comrade George B. Fielder Department Commander. The Seventeenth Encampment, held in Trenton January 30, 1884, elected Comrade Henry M. Nevins Department Commander, and re-elected him at the Encampment held in Trenton, February 11 1885. The Nineteenth Encampment, held in Trenton February 11, 1886, elected Comrade Frank O. Cole Department Commander. The Twentieth Encampment, held in Trenton February 10, 1887, elected Comrade John L. Wheeler Department Commander. The Twenty-first Encampment, held in Trenton February 9, 1888, elected Comrade E. Burd Grub Department Commander, who has been untiring in his efforts to advance the honor and promote the welfare of our order, and for the surprising results which have followed his unselfish labor, the comrades of the Department of New Jersey will ever feel grateful. The Twenty-second Encampment, held in Trenton February 11, 1889, elected Comrade William W. D. Miller, who is at present in command of this Department.

New Jersey was the first State in the Union to establish a home for her soldiers and sailors The Hon. Marcus L. Ward, of this city, was untiring in his labors in their behalf, and through his efforts the Legislature enacted a resolution approved March 23, 1865, for its establish-ment. The home was opened on July 4, 1866. The usefulness of the institution is shown by the fact that over 14,724 veterans have been housed, fed, clothed and cared for. The cost of maintenance has been $32,592.79 yearly. This department, in 1886, petitioned the Legislature for an appropriation to erect new buildings to replace those that by long use had become unfit for their purpose. The Legislature promptly appropriated $60,000, and then increased the amount to $125,000. A beautiful site on the eastern shore of the Passaic River was selected, in Kearney township (named after General Phil. Kearney), and near his home, in Hudson county. The grounds cover seventeen acres. The old mansion on the place was remodeled and six new building erected, all especially designed for that use by Comrade Paul G. Boticher, architect. The Hon. Marcus L. Ward has been treasurer of the home for eighteen years, and since his death this position has been filled by his son, Marcus L. Ward, Jr. Comrade Peter F. Rodgers is the present superintendent, and has discharged the duties of his position satisfactorily during the past nine years. The chaplain, Rev. Isaac Tuttle, a comrade of Post No. 1, has served continually since the opening of the home.

New Jersey has made liberal provisions for her soldiers and sailors in addition to the State Home. A relief is frequently extended to indigent veterans at their homes by a pay-ment of from two to six dollars per month, according to the circumstances in each case, and in this way nearly $200,000 have been disbursed. Provision has also been made for the burial of any honorably discharged soldier or sailor who may die without leaving means for funeral expenses. Such interment is not to be made in any cemetery or plot used exclusively for the interment of the pauper dead. The cost for interment is not to exceed $35, and an additional sum of $15 is allowed for a headstone.

A fine bronze statue of General Philip Kearney stands in Military Park, and was erected through the efforts of comrades of Kearney Post, No. 1. The comrades of Phil. Sheridan Post are considering ways and means of erecting a suitable monument to the memory of Phil. Sheridan in one of the parks.

"Memorial Day" is a legal holiday in New Jersey.

FREDERICK S. FISH,

COUNSELLOR AT LAW,

770 BROAD STREET,

NEWARK, N. J.

FRANK HOLT & CO.,

Practical Watchmakers and Jewelers,

DIAMONDS

NO. 6 ACADEMY STREET,

Opp. Post Office, one door above Broad St.,

And 155 Springfield Avenue, - - NEWARK, N. J.

E. T. HART BOX CO.,

MANUFACTURERS OF—

PAPER BOXES

Nos. 261 & 263 Market Street,

COR. LAWRENCE STREET,

NEWARK, N. J.

H. P. COOK. A. V. C. GENUNG.

COOK & GENUNG,

MASONS' MATERIALS

Standard Hard Pipe and Coal,

MAIN OFFICE AND YARD, 16 & 18 JERSEY STREET,

BRANCH YARD, ASTOR ST. AND R. R. AVE.,

NEWARK, N. J.

HOW A MAN SHOULD BE JUDGED.

Who shall judge a man from nature?
  Who shall know him by his dress?
Paupers may be fit for princes,
  Princes fit for something less.
Crumpled shirt and dirty jacket
  May beclothe the golden ore
Of the deepest thought and feeling—
  Satin vest could do no more.

There are springs of crystal nectar
  Ever swelling out of stone;
There are purple buds and golden,
  Hidden, crushed, and overgrown,
God, who counts by souls, not dresses,
  Loves and prospers you and me;
While He values thrones the highest
  But as pebbles in the sea.

Man, upraised above his fellows
  Oft forgets his fellows then;
Masters—rulers lords, remember,
  That your meanest hands are men!
Men of labor, men of feeling,
  Men by thought and men by fame,
Claiming equal rights to sunshine
  In a man's ennobling name.

There are foam-embroidered oceans,
  There are little weed-clad rills,
There are feeble, inch-high saplings,
  There are cedars on the hills;
God, who counts by souls, not stations,
  Loves and prospers you and me;
For to him all vain distinctions,
  Are as pebbles in the sea.

Toiling hands alone are builders
  Of a nation's wealth and fame;
Titled laziness is pensioned,
  Fed, and fattened on the same;
By the sweat of others' foreheads,
  Living only to rejoice,
While the poor man's outraged freedom
  Vainly lifteth up its voice.

Truth and justice are eternal,
  Born with loveliness and light;
Secret wrong shall never prosper
  While there is a starry night.
God, whose world-heard voice is singing
  Boundless love to you and me,
Sink oppression with its titles,
  As the pebbles in the sea.

THE fitness of things: Foggs—"Just look at that absurd hat. Why it's as tall as a steeple." Boggs—"What's odd about that? Isn't there a belle under it?"

MISS GOTHAM—"I adore traveling. Where you ever in Greece, Miss Loin?" Miss Loin, of Cincinnati—"No, I never was; but papa was in that lard trust, you know."

CUSTOMER—"Say, Rothstein, who's that man doing all that yelling and screaming and swearing at the clerks in the rear part of the store?" Rothstein—"Oh, dot vos Rosenberg, der silent pardner."

FIRST GAMIN—"Say, I'll bet you a nickel I've got more money in my pocket than you have." Second Gamin—"Go yer once." After money is put up: First Gamin—"How much money have you got in my pockets?"

MRS. O'FLAHERTY—"Have yez any tin quart pails, Misther Doogan?" Mr. Doogan—"No, Mrs. O'Flaherty, but Oi have plinty av tin wan quart pails. Mrs. O'Flaherty—"An' that's what Oi axed yez for, Mr. Doogan."

"PLEASE, ma'am, will you give me an old suit of your husband's clothes? I am one of the Johnstown flood sufferers." "Poor man! Of course I will. Come right in. So you were in that dreadful flood, were you?" "No, ma'am, but my wife sent all my clothes to the people who were."

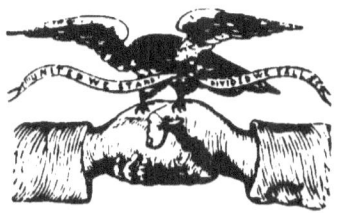

Sketch of Phil. Sheridan Post.

BY THE POST ADJUTANT.

PHIL. SHERIDAN POST, No. 110, G. A. R., Department of New Jersey, was organized December 6, 1888, with 21 charter members; its present membership is 140. The following comrades are its officers: Post Commander, Henry L. Hallock; Senior Vice, William Nichols, Jr.; Vice, George W. Dunn; Adjutant, Howard Thomas; Quartermaster, Andrew M. Grey; Officer of the Day, Robert Johnson; Officer of Guard, John W. Keller; Post Surgeon, Henry D. Cozzens; Chaplain, O. R. Olds. The regular meetings are held every Thursday evening in their rooms, corner of Ferry and McWhorter streets. The object of the association is to render all the assistance in its power towards relieving worthy members and assisting the orphans and widows of its departed comrades, as far as its means will permit. Soldiers and sailors who have been honorably discharged from the service of the United States, who have not as yet attached themselves to any other Post of the G. A. R., are cordially invited to unite with the Post in advancing the great principles of the organization. Fraternity to our comrades, charity towards our fellow-creatures, and loyalty to our country. The Grand Army of the Republic is one of the noblest associations in existence, and aside from its benevolent and humane characteristics, one that cannot fail to lift mankind up to a higher standard of moral excellence. The order is grand and noble. Its precepts are sublime, and its symbols are replete with instructions both elevating and salutary. Yes, comrades, fall in, and though day by day the great enemy may be picking off, one by one, of those who first enlisted, let those of us in the ranks be encouraged by the new recruits that come forward to take their places.

> " Fall in, fall in, old comrades,"
> And fight our battles o'er,
> Until above the last low bier,
> The wings of freedom soar:
> Stand hand to hand and heart to heart,
> In Fame's eternal care,
> Until the great reunion
> Unites us over there.

To our patrons enquiry is sometimes made, "Why these entertainments?" To all such we reply that the Grand Army of the Republic has distributed nearly $2,000,000 in charity. This amount has been divided among 66,876 destitute soldiers and sailors and their widows and orphans. Of this amount the Department of New Jersey has contributed over $25,000. Thus it will be seen that the main objects of the organization are to comfort the afflicted, relieve the distressed and assist those who are needy, thereby sending a ray of sunshine into the life of those whose paths are overshadowed in gloom. The officers and members of Phil. Sheridan Post, No. 110, desire to avail themselves of the present opportunity and gratefully return thanks to all their public-spirited fellow-citizens who have contributed in any manner towards the success of this, their first entertainment.

The attention of our friends and the readers of this programme is respectfully called to the business advertisements to be found on its various pages. Without the assistance so generously given by these enterprising business men the book could not have been published.

HENRY L. HALLOCK, Commander Phil. Sheridan Post, No. 110.
HOWARD THOMAS, Adjutant.

KEARNY

UNDER THE STATUE.

BY S. J. SIMONS.

COMRADE SIMONS, who lives in Massachusetts, visited this city two years ago on a business tour, stopping at the Park House. One evening he leisurely strolled through Military Park and beholding the monument erected to the memory of New Jersey's "hero," Gen. Phil Kearny, he wrote the following poem, which appears in print for the first time. The cut has been generously furnished by J. Watts Kearny.

A stranger in the city,
　Far from friends and home,
I chanced one pleasant evening
　Into your park to roam ;
I watched the youth and maiden
　As they passed with love and pride,
Then I thought of distant dear ones,
　And bowed my head and sighed.

At last by intuition,
　Or by some unseen hand,
My attention was arrested
　By a figure calm and grand.
My vision gently lifted,
　And lo, to my surprise,
I saw my old commander,
　And the mist it filled my eyes.

Yes, there stood noble Kearny,
　The jewel in the crown
Of all those great commanders
　Who put rebellion down.
I gazed on those stern features,
　And my old heart gave a thrill,
As back by Kearny's side I stood
　On Malvern's bloody hill.

And then I thought of Fair Oaks,
　And Sunday at Seven Pines,
When Kearny, with his gallant boys,
　Broke through the rebel lines ;
When, had he been supported,
　(As the rebels since have said)
Fewer the years of bloody war,
　And less of Union dead.

Once more I stood with Kearny
　On Malvern's fiery height
Where another got the credit,
　But where Kearny won the fight ;
And then before my vision,
　Chantelly's wood appears,
But I could not see the statue,
　My eyes were filled with tears.

General ✛ Grant,

MARSHALL is universally recognized, both in this country
and Europe, as at the head of Engravers on steel. His
Washington, Lincoln and Longfellow
are all of the highest art.

PRINTED in TWO EDITIONS, CELLULOID ᴬᴺᴰ INDIA PAPER

Approved by the Family of Gen. Grant.

" My mother and family have examined with great care Mr. Marshall's new portrait of my father, General Grant. We all agree that as a portrait it is a good one. That it is a work of art, Marshall's name is a guarantee."   F. D. GRANT."

March 31, 1885.

" It is excellent; I do not see how it could be improved.
                                        U. S. GRANT, Jr.

It is the Only Steel Line Engraving of General Grant Published.

PUBLISHERS,

CURRIER & JONES.

Enthusiastic Opinions of Intimate Friends of General Grant.

Hon. ROBERT T. LINCOLN, son of Abraham Lincoln: "It is an excellent likeness and a fine work of art."

Hon. JOHN SHERMAN, Senator from Ohio: "It is certainly very excellent, both as a portrait and as a work of art."

GEO. W. CHILDS, Esq., of Philadelphia: "It is the best and strongest portrait of General Grant I have ever seen.

Senator JOHN A. LOGAN: "Beautiful, unquestionably a fine likeness, and as a work of art exceedingly good."

Major-General O. O. HOWARD: "As a work of art I think the portrait superb. To me, he looks in this picture as he looked when President."

Major-General H. W. SLOCUM: "I regard Marshall's new portrait as excellent in every respect."

WHITELAW REID, Esq., Ed. N. Y. *Tribune:* "It is certainly a faithful and satisfactory likeness."

Ex-Pres. RUTHERFORD B. HAYES: "Marshall's new Portrait is certainly very fine."

Lieut-Gen'l W. T. SHERMAN: "The certificate of Col. Fred. Grant is all that is needed for Marshall's New Steel Portrait of General Grant."

D. HUNTINGTON, Esq., Pres National Academy of Design: "It is rich, strong, and broad in effect, and preserves the essential traits with vigor."

GEORGE WILLIAM CURTIS, Esq.: "It is by far the best likeness of him as he appears in these latter days that I have seen, and it is very fortunate that so admirable a portrait has been obtained."

Hon. ROSCOE CONKLING: "It is to me really a very satisfactory and life-like portrait."

Senator GEO. F. EDMUNDS: "This new portait I admire. I wish it to hang up in my house."

NEW YORK, August 20, 1885.

MESSRS. CURRIER & JONES,

Gentlemen:—I have always considered Marshall's portraits above reproach, but in printing his steel engraving of General Grant, by your new process, upon celluloid, you have brought out the strength and richness of his work far better than it has ever been done before. Having acted as private stenographer to the General, I can testify, that besides being a work of art, it is an admirable likeness.   Respectfully,

FRED. J. HALL.

On Sunday, April 5, 1885, when he thought he could not live through the day, General Grant signed five copies of this new portrait, which Mr. Marshall had brought at the request of the family. These signed portraits General Grant then presented, one copy each, to General Bedeau, Ex-Senator Chaffee, Rev. Dr. Newman, and his physicians, Drs. Douglass and Shrady.   CURRIER & JONES.

NEWARK, N. J.

Testimonials.

...

NEW MADISON, OHIO, DRAKE COUNTY, Aug. 8, 1885.

COLONEL FRED. D. GRANT,

Sir:—I would be pleased to find out where I could get the best Portraits and good Engravings of your Father, GENERAL U. S. GRANT. Please hand this to one of the Engraving Companies in New York, they can answer me, and oblige a soldier.

Yours respectfully,

[Referred to us by Colonel Grant.]   HARRY MILLER.

BROOKLYN, September 5, 1885.

MESSRS. CURRIER & JONES, NEWARK, N. J.:

Thank you for the portrait of General Grant (on celluloid) received to-day. It is a beautiful work of art and a good likeness; Mr. Marshall has never been more successful than in this instance, I should say. General Grant's face is impressed on my memory, having seen it for the first time just after the fall of Vicksburg when he came among us in Tennessee as a conqueror, and, naturally, was a person of much interest. I will value the picture and again thank you for it.

LAURA C. HOLLOWAY.

THE ART CRITIC OF THE *Brooklyn Eagle* WRITES AS FOLLOWS:

A new portrait of General Grant has been published by Currier & Jones, of Newark, that commands more than ordinary attention. It is a fine engraving by William E. Marshall, representing the General in civilian dress, facing almost full to the front. It is a capital likeness, and those who saw him in the last years of his Presidency will accede to that fact. The expression is quiet, but the eyes are alive, alert and thoughtful, giving the face the aspect of strength in repose, and the head and bust are accurately molded. The tone is low, but sharply broken by the high lights, thereby giving power as well as richness to the work. Around the oval that is occupied by the portrait is the simulation of a mat, or frame, filled with an Arabesque pattern remarkable in its detail. The notable feature of the engraving, however, is that it is printed on celluloid, with the best results. It has almost the appearance of Japanese paper, but gives to the lines a clearness and, to the high lights, a silvery brightness that paper could not impart. It will be no surprising result of this publication if celluloid should be quite generally used, in place of Japan and India papers, for proof etchings and engravings. Its vindication as a medium is ample in the case of Mr. Marshall's portrait.

CURRIER & JONES,

Publishers,

NEWARK. N. J.

—38—

IN ACTION.

Fun in Battle.

By Comrade Wm. Nichols.

HUMOROUS things were always occurring on the battle-field. At Malvern Hill a Confederate colonel ran ahead of his regiment, and, discovering his men were not following him, uttered a fierce oath and exclaimed:

"Come on! Do you want to live forever?" (Laughter.)

The appeal was irresistible, and many a poor fellow who had laughed at the colonel's queer exhortation, laid down his life soon after.

One of our brave men, Jim Stillman, was badly wounded in the Chantilly fight which killed Phil. Kearney. The next day we took Jim, who was a good Christian, to the Washington Hospital, where he eventually died. After his death our chaplain, who knew Jim was a devout Christian, went over to the hospital to hear about his last hours.

"So Stillman is dead!" he said to the good-natured English nurse. "I should so have liked to have spoken to him once more to soothe his dying moments. Did he die happily?"

"O, yes, said the unregenerate nurse, "I soothed his last moments as best I could myself."

"What did you say to him?" asked the chaplain.

"O, I talked very soothing to him."

"'Jim,' sez I, 'you're mortal bad.' 'I am,' sez'e.

'Jim,' sez I, 'I don't think you'll get better.' 'No,' sez'e.

'Jim,' sez I, 'you're going fast.' 'Yes,' sez'e.

'Jim, says I, 'I don't think soldiers can 'ope to go to 'eaven?' 'Do you think so,' sez'e.

'Perhaps, Jim, sez I, 'you may go to 'ell.'

'Perhaps so,' sez'e.

'Jim,' sez I, 'you ought to be very grateful as there's a place pervided for you, and that you've got somewhere to go to, and I think 'e 'eard me, sir, and then 'e smiled and died.'"

"This," continued Comrade Nichols, "reminds me of the experience of Chaplain Twitchell of the Fifth Connecticut. Chaplain Twitchell is now Mark Twain's clergyman, and, they say, does a good deal of the humorist's thinking. "There was in my regiment," says Twitchell, "a splendid soldier by the name of Corporal Jones. The corporal fought himself down to a skeleton and finally went to the hospital. On recovering from his dangerous sickness I felt it my duty to have a serious pastoral talk with him, and while he convalesced I watched for an opportunity for it. As I sat one day on the side of his bed in the

[Continued on Page 44.

FIRST

GRAND GIFT ENTERTAINMENT

—OF—

Phil × Sheridan × Post, × 110

G. A. R., DEPT. OF N. J.,

On which occasion will be produced the most successful and funniest of Hoyt's Comedies, as performed over 350 nights in New York City, A

BUNCH OF KEYS;

OR, THE HOTEL

Under the Management of Mr. Gus Bothner,

— AT —

JACOBS' GRAND OPERA HOUSE,

ON —

Monday Evening, November 11, 1889.

ADMISSION, $1.00.   NO RESERVED SEATS.

It is a collection of incidents intended to teach no moral in particular, stirred together by Charles H. Hoyt, incited, aided and abetted by Willie Edouin. The piece is called a comedy, because comedy is the word used to describe almost everything put upon the stage at present, and the authors desire to avoid the charge of eccentricity, having enough else to answer for. The people who risk their lives, limbs and reputation in presenting the piece and the characters they are alleged to assume, may be learned by a careful study of the following:

✧ PROGRAMME ✧

INDIVIDUALS IN ACT I.

TEDDY KEYS, a wild rosebud, with the accompaning thorns..........ADA BOTHNER
ROSE KEYS, her sister, also of the rose variety, but full-blown and rather of
    the prim-rose order....................................LILLA LINDEN
MAY KEYS, also a sister of Teddy, the third and last of a Bunch of Keys;...
                               BLANCHE SEYMOUR
DOLLY DOBBS, a singular domestic—that is, she "breaks no crockery"....
                            GERTRUDE STANWOOD
MATILDA JENKINS, searching for her lost one......................LILLIAN WADE
GILLY SPOONER, a rural masher, engaged to Rose........CHARLES F. RAYMOND
JONAS GRIMES, a brakeman, who is one of Nature's noblemen—this is the
    author's ideal of a perfect man—watch him...... .....JAMES B. MACKIE
TOM HARDING, May's lover......................................GUS P. THOMAS
SAM FOSS, looking for a job—and gets one.......................WILLIAM SMITH
LITTLETON SNAGGS, ESQ., a legal gentleman, who knows as much of run-
    ning a hotel as a good many in that business do..........CHARLES BURKE

DISGUISES ASSUMED IN ACTS II. AND III.

J. FRISK, Sr., a dealer in lightning rods.. }
J. ROCKFORD SMITH, a drummer...... } ....TOM HARDING
COL. ST. CLAIR BRAY, a politician. }
ROSE KEYS....................... } ....GILLY SPOONER
MISS EMMA POUGHKEEPSIE, operatic artist.........................ROSE KEYS
SIGNORINA JERSECITY, operatic artist..............................MAY KEYS
ST. LAWRENCE JENKINS, a drummer.............................TEDDY KEYS
PLUG MULDOON, a Sullivanite.....................................SAM FOSS

SYNOPSIS OF SCENERY AND INCIDENTS.

THE WILL. ACT. I.—Anxiety of the Keys family. Arrival of Littleton Snaggs. Reading of the Will. Concealment of the codicil. Snaggs opens the Grand View Hotel as possession is nine points of the law. Teddy volunteers to assist, much to the disgust of the Keys family.

THE HOTEL. THE FUNNIEST OF FUNNY SCENES. ACT II.—Hotel opened. Enough provisions for a regiment. "I'll run it according to law." We must see the Will They try the safe. "Grimes, remember the bell." Teddy's desire to give a ball. Guests arrive. Opera singers, politician, lightning rod agent. "Have a drink?" Matilda's search. The proposal. Snaggs not drunk, but sleepy. The suicide.

HOTEL AFTER A STORM. ACT III.—More guests. "He's a pugilist." Arrival of a supposed drummer. The plot exposed. Success of the Keys family. Recovery of the codicil. Arrival of the real drummer. The decision. Consternation of Snaggs. Matilda's victory. "Good-bye."

George Chenet ....Business Manager
Watty Hydes..Musical Director
William Smith...Stage Manager

The Orchestra, under the direction of Mr. J. L. Cusson, will perform the following selections:

"Le Pere De La Victoire".......................................Ganne
Selection—Operatic...G. Wiegand
Waltz—"In the Clouds"...Waldteufel
March—"Monte Christo, Jr.".....................................G. Wiegand

MAJ.-GEN. GEORGE B. McCLELLAN.

hospital tent chatting with him, he asked me what the spring campaign was going to be. I told him that I didn't know."

"Well," said he, "I suppose that General McClellan knows all about it." "General McClellan," I said, "has his plans, of course, but he doesn't *know*. Things may not turn out as he expects."

"But," said the corporal, "President Lincoln knows, doesn't he?"

"No," I said, "he doesn't know either. He has his ideas, but he can't see ahead any more than General McClellan can."

"Dear me," said the corporal, "it would be a great comfort if there was somebody that did know about these things," and I saw my chance.

"True, corporal," I observed, "that's a very natural feeling; and the blessed fact is there is One who does know everything, both past and future, about you and me, and about this army; who knows when we are going to move, and where to, and what's going to happen; knows the whole thing."

"Oh," says the corporal, "you mean old Scott!" (Laughter.)

"Jokes."

BY COMRADE COZZENS.

THE Teuton is often a long time in learning American idioms. One who had been here for a year or more, and who could speak some English before his arrival, a very short and corpulent man, by the way, went to his grocer's and paid a bill which had been standing for several weeks.

"Now you are all square, Hans."

"I vas vat?"

"You are square, I said."

"I vas square."

"Yes, you are all square now."

Hans was silent for a moment, then with reddening face and flashing eyes he brought his plump fist down upon the counter and said:

"See here, mine frent, I vil haf no more peezness mit you. I treat you like a shentleman, I pay my pill, und you make a shoke of me—you say I vas square ven I know I was round as a parrel. I dond like such shokes. My peezness mit you vas done."

COMRADES afflicted with baldness should rub their heads with a piece of steel; you are all aware that steel makes the "Hair Spring."

A Battle Field Scene.

SELECTED BY COMRADE LEARY.

AFTER the battle, in an enclosed lot near York street, Gettysburg, was found a corpse in Federal blue, near a small stream of water. Tightly grasped in the dead soldier's hand was the likeness of three sweet, innocent little children. On them his last gaze had been fastened, as, alone and unattended, on the dreary field of slaughter, his soul had departed to its God. He was buried at the time in a lot of Judge Russell's, near where he had been found.

Thousands of copies of the picture were widely circulated, and at length one reached Cattaraugus county, N. Y., and was there recognized as a likeness of the three children of a man named Hummiston. He had left his humble home to enlist in the 154th N. Y., belonging to Coster's brigade of the 11th Corps. He had been killed while Coster was trying to save the line of retreat.

The remains of Orderly Sergeant Hummiston now rest in grave No. 14, section B., of the New York lot in the National Cemetery. A prize of fifty dollars was offered for the best poem on this touching incident. The award was made to J. G. Clark for the following thrilling stanzas: (Tune, "Tattoo," or "A Watcher, Pale and Tearful.")

Upon the field of Gettysburg,
  The summer sun was high,
When freedom met her Southern foe
  Beneath a Northern sky;
Among the heroes of the North,
  Who swelled her grand array—
Who rushed, like mountain eagles forth,
  From happy homes away.

There stood a man of humble fame,
  A sire of children, three,
And gazed, within a little frame,
  Their pictured forms to see;
And blame him not if, in the strife,
  He breathed a soldier's prayer—
"O! Father, guard the soldier's wife,
  And for his children care."

Upon the field of Gettysburg
  When morning shone again,
The crimson cloud of battle burst
  In streams of fiery rain;
Our legions quelled the awful flood
  Of shot, and steel, and shell,
While banners, marked with ball and blood,
  Around them rose and fell;

And none more nobly won the name
  Of Champion of the Free,
Than he who pressed the little frame
  That held his children three;
And none were braver in the strife
  Than he who breathed the prayer:
"O! Father, guard the soldier's wife,
  And for his children care."

Upon the field of Gettysburg
  The full moon slowly rose,
She looked, and saw ten thousand brows
  All pale in death's repose;
And down beside a silver stream,
  From other forms away,
Calm as a warrior in a dream,
  Our fallen comrade lay.

His limbs were cold, his sightless eyes
  Were fixed upon the three
Sweet stars that rose in memory's skies,
  To light him o'er death's sea.
Then honored be the soldier's life,
  And hallowed be his prayer:
"O! Father, guard the soldier's wife,
  And for his orphans care."

HEADQUARTERS ON THE BATTLEFIELD.

Woman's Relief Corps.

THE first organization of the Woman's Relief Corps was formed in Portland, Maine, in 1869. This society of women is actively engaged in the good work voluntarily assumed 20 years ago, and deserves the highest praise for the honorable stand it has chosen amongst the numerous similar associations since formed, and which have so generously aided the Grand Army of the Republic in the relief of unfortunate and needy comrades and their families. The National Encampment of the G. A. R. gave them official recognition in 1881; a resolution approving the work of the Woman's Relief Corps was unanimously adopted. Comrade Lovering was authorized to correspond with these societies and encourage them in their good work. A national organization was formed at Denver on July 25th, 1883; Mrs. E. Florence Barker was chosen President and Mrs. Kate B. Sherwood Secretary. The objects of the association are to specially aid and assist the Grand Army of the Republic and to perpetuate the memory of their heroic dead, to assist such union soldiers and sailors as need our help and protection, and to extend needful aid to their widows and orphans, to find homes and employment and assure them of sympathy and friends, to cherish and emulate the deeds of our army nurses, and of all loyal women who rendered loving service to their country in her hour of peril, to inculcate lessons of patriotism and love of country among our children and in the communities in which we live, to maintain true allegiance to the United States of America, to discountenance whatever tends to weaken loyalty, and to encourage the spread of universal liberty and equal rights to all men. The society has at present a membership of sixty-four thousand ladies and have expended for relief over $170,000. This is certainly a magnificent showing of the executive ability of the ladies of the relief corps in organization. The moneys expended for relief were either contributed directly to the relief funds of posts, or were personally disbursed by individual members or committees of the Woman's Relief Corps on visits to families of soldiers and sailors. Large as is the amount thus expended for relief, it does not fully show the worth of this auxiliary to the Grand Army of the Republic, the cheering visits to the homes of the afflicted, the consoling hours spent by the bedside of sick and dying veterans by the ladies of this association, cannot be adequately measured by any money standard, nor can a full appreciation of their loving work on behalf of suffering humanity be properly expressed in words.

THE small boy who had been watching through the stove-pipe hole the antics of a loving couple, ran down to the kitchen in high glee to describe the whole proceeding to his little sister.

"Oh, it's such fun," said he, in conclusion.

"What is such fun?" asked his mother, who had just entered.

"Why, to play lunatic asylum like Sister Bertie and Mr. Snipes are doing in the parlor."

"WHAT DID THE PRIVATES DO?"

BY COMRADE S. M.

What did the privates do? Their work
  Lies far beyond our kin ;
For history does not record
  The deeds of private men.
We read about Thermopylæ
  And its one hero brave ;
And tho' he had three hundred men,
  Each one is in his grave.

His name, also; but one survives—
  The great Leonidas.
He carries all the honors off
  For guarding that long pass.
His men are known as they would be
  Were they three hundred steeds.
Their names are lost in his. Perhaps
  'Tis all a private needs.

Napoleon and Wellington
  Fought Waterloo, they say ;
But who can tell a private's name
  Who perished there that day?
They are not marked on history's page
  Nor yet in epics sung ;
Their leaders all the glory get
  Of noble deeds they've done.

One private, only one, is known,
  Of all that ancient throng ;
A poet (thoughtlessly, no doubt,)
  Embalmed his name in song—
" Ben Battles was a soldier bold,"
  Alas, he lost his legs !
And then the bard makes fun, because
  He walked on wooden pegs.

Such is the cold world's gratitude
  To these who fight her wars ;
She bows her head to epaulettes,
  But maimed men she abhors.
I heard a general talking, once,
  (I shuddered when he spake.)
A call was made for volunteers
  Some dangerous place to take.

He thought he saw promotion there ;
  Such are the rules of war.
He said, he lost most all his men,
  But, then, he won his star.
What? was he braver than those men ?
  No, not a whit more brave !
But what won they ? They bullets won,
  Wounds, or a nameless grave.

What did the privates do, indeed !
  Ah, they were gath'ing scars.
And helping some great officer
  To shoulder-straps and stars.
I'll whisper it, but don't you tell.
  Privates are the backbone,
For what would Appomatox be
  Had Grant stood there alone ?

-50

Lieut., Major, Lieut.-Col., Col. and Gen. E. B. Grubb.

BY A COMRADE OF PHIL. SHERIDAN POST.

A BORN SOLDIER. No need of military or training school. It came natural, a gift born in him. Surrounded by all the comforts and luxuries that wealth could afford, he was one of the first to respond to his country's call. He enlisted in the 3d New Jersey Regiment as Second Lieutenant. I remember what a fine and gallant looking officer he made ; soon promoted to the rank of First Lieutenant, and then appointed to a position on General Taylor's staff. The brigade, after passing through many severe engagements and being greatly reduced in numbers, our regiment (the 23d N. J.) was sent to join the brigade, and, arriving at the front, Grubb rode out to meet us, and seeing so many familiar faces and such a large regiment, he remarked, " O, how I would like to be Colonel of that regiment." It was but a short time before he was in command, and he was no prouder than we.

Well do I remember our first engagement, the battle of Fredericksburg. My feelings I never could describe, but we all felt as long as he was in sight and command, we would come out all right, and it was due to him that after our right had been so cut up, that it was rallied and led into the thickest of the fight. At Chancellorsville he was always at the head of his regiment until his horse was shot, and then on foot leading his men, and the last to retire from the field. His kindness to his men was remarkable, always on the lookout for their comfort, and not too proud to enter their tents and see how they fared. At regimental or dress parade or inspection, we felt so proud, for there was no other officer who could compare with him, either in mount, riding or dress; the gayest and bravest of them all. When our term of service had expired he took us home to Beverly, and before we were mustered out he volunteered and went to Harrisburg to help repel General Lee who threatened to invade Pennsylvania. His services, however, were not required, and returning to Beverly, the regiment was disbanded. He did not stop here, but recruited and sent to the front the 34th and afterwards raised the 37th, and reporting to General Butler, did good service at the siege of Petersburg. It was there I had the pleasure of meeting him again, our regiment, 1st N. J. cavalry, (for I had re-enlisted), was marching by his camp at midnight, being very tired I rode to his tent, walked in, and was used like a general ; had a good dose of commissary, lunch and a good cigar, with a cordial invitation to call again whenever I was near, and I only a private. In March, 1865, he was made " Brevet Brigadier General of the Volunteers," a title well earned.

His interest in military affairs did not cease here. He commanded the 6th Regiment National Guard of New Jersey, was Captain of City troops of Philadelphia, and was elected Commander of the Grand Army of the Republic, Department of New Jersey, in which he always took great interest.

Phil. Sheridan Post, No. 110, was the last post he mustered in, and he terms it his baby, and a fine, large, healthy baby it has grown to be. Like a fond parent, he cannot do enough for it ; he has presented it with a large and valuable silk American flag besides other valuable gifts, and the baby is glad it was born.

Abraham Lincoln.

WHY SHOULD THE SPIRIT OF MORTAL BE PROUD?

PRESIDENT LINCOLN'S FAVORITE POEM.

Oh! why should the spirit of mortal be proud?
Like a swift floating meteor, a fast-flying cloud,
A flash of the lightning, a break of the wave,
Man passeth from life to rest in the grave.

The leaves of the oak and willow shall fade,
Be scattered around and together be laid;
And the young and the old, and the low and the high,
Should moulder to dust and together shall lie.

The infant and mother, attended and loved;
The mother that infant's affection who proved,
The husband that mother and infant who blessed,
Each, all are away to their dwellings of rest.

The maid on whose cheek, on whose brow, in whose eye,
Shone beauty and pleasure, her triumphs are by;
And the memory of those who loved her and praised,
Are alike from the minds of the living erased.

The hand of the king that the sceptre hath borne,
The brow of the priest that the mitre hath worn;
The eye of the sage and the heart of the brave,
Are hidden and lost in the depths of the grave.

The peasant, whose lot was to sow and to reap,
The herdsman, who climbed with his goats up the steep,
The beggar who wandered in search for his bread,
Have faded away like the grass that we tread.

The saint who enjoyed the communion of heaven,
The sinner who dared to remain unforgiven,
The wise and the foolish, the guilty and just,
Have quietly mingled their bones in the dust;

So the multitude goes, like the flower or the weed,
That withers away to let others succeed;
So the multitude comes, even those we behold,
To repeat every tale that has often been told!

. 5:4 .

For we are the same our fathers have been;
We see the same sights our fathers have seen;
We drink the same stream and view the same sun,
And run the same course our fathers have run.

The thoughts we are thinking our fathers would think;
From the death we are shrinking our fathers would shrink,
To the life we are clinging they also would cling;
But it speeds from us all like a bird on the wing.

They loved, but the story we cannot untold;
They scorned, but the heart of the haughty is cold;
They grieved, but no wail from their slumber will come;
They joyed, but the tongue of their gladness is dumb.

They died; aye! they died; we things that are now,
That walk on the turf that lies over their brow,
And make in their dwellings a transient abode,
Meet the things that they meet on their pilgrimage road.

Yea! hope and despondency, pleasure and pain,
We mingle together in sunshine and rain;
And the smile and the tear, the song and the dirge,
Still follow each other, like surge upon surge.

'Tis the wink of an eye, 'tis the draught of a breath,
From the blossom of health to the paleness of death,
From the gilded saloon to the bier and the shroud!
Oh! why should the spirit of mortal be proud?

How George Was Captured.

"YOU look very much excited, dear," he said, when she entered the parlor, where he was waiting for her.

"Well, I should think I ought to look excited," she answered. "I've just had the most awful argument with ma."

And she began to weep hysterically.

"Why, what is the matter, my darling?" he inquired, as he slid his arm around her waist and endeavored to soothe her. "What was the argument?"

"Oh, how can I tell you? She said you were only trifling with me, and that you would never pop the question; and I told her she did you a great injustice, for I believed that you would pop the question to-night. She said you wouldn't, and I said you would, and we had it hot and heavy. Dear George, you will not let ma triumph over me, will you?"

"Wh-hy, certainly not," answered George.

"I knew it, my darling!" the dear girl exclaimed; "come, let us go to ma and tell her how much mistaken she was."

And they did, and ma didn't seem to be so very much broken down over the affair after all.

"Memorial Day."

MEMORIAL DAY, which falls on the 30th of May of each year, with its tender and beautiful ceremonies, is now generally and fittingly observed throughout the entire country. It was designed to perpetuate and cherish the memory of our heroic dead, who in manhood's hours made their breasts a shield between our Union and its foes. Their soldier lives were the reveille of emancipation to a race of our fellow-creatures in bondage, and their deaths the tattoo of traitors in arms against our glorious inheritance. As we gather around their sacred mounds and mark them with the dear old flag they saved from dishonor, let us renew our pledges to aid and assist those whom they have left amongst us—the widow and orphan.

> Mounds of our heroes, keep sacred their graves.
> As gently the grasses the summer wind waves
> Though plain be their headstone, yet sad is the tear
> That falls from the loved ones o'er the brave volunteer
> Here sleep the heroes who for freedom were brave,
> Dear to the nation are her soldier boy's grave

DECORATION.

Gather the choicest flowers.
Strew them o'er the brave,
Let them fall like gentle showers,
Upon each veteran's grave.

They bravely fought and fell
On many a Southern plain,
Upholding our starry emblem well
On the battlefields of fame

All o'er our honored sod,
On the waves of every sea
Flutters again the grand old flag
Proud emblem of the free

Then bring your rarest flowers,
And cover the hero's grave,
Who fought in manhood's hours
Our beautiful land to save

→⚡MATTIA × BROTHERS←⚡

Successors to R. H. GREEN,

PHOTOGRAPHERS AND ARTISTS,

773 BROAD STREET, NEWARK, N. J.

SILVER MEDALS AND FIRST AND SECOND PREMIUMS

Awarded to us for the Finest Display of

PORTRAITS, CRAYONS AND PASTELS,

At the late State Fair, at Waverly, N. J.

Reduced rates to the G. A. R. members. RATES LOW AND SATISFAC-TION GUARANTEED.

Owing to pressing business we shall keep the Gallery open for the accommodation of our patrons from 7 A. M. to 9 P. M. until January 30th, 1890; Sundays, from 8 A. M. to 5 P. M.

MATTIA BROTHERS,

⚡LEADING ⚡ PHOTOGRAPHERS ⚡ AND ⚡ ARTISTS⚡

773 Broad Street, ⚡⚡ Newark, N. J.

To sketch the human face divine,
And draw the life-like portrait fine,
And stamp the features as displayed
In every tint and every shade;
This is their art and well they can
Thus represent the youth of man,
The peerless beauty, aged dame
Or lovely matron all the same.
And babies' pictures nice and cute,
The dry-plate makes them just to suit.
Mattia Brothers pictures are all first-class,
Their prices are never to dear,
Then get your pictures taken there.

We enlarge Portraits in Crayon, Pastel, India Ink and Oil Painting. We sell all kinds of Picture Frames at the lowest prices.

MATTIA BROTHERS, 773 BROAD ST., NEWARK, N. J.

"Heroism in Peace as well as in War."

BY COMRADE BAKER.

IN 1866 cholera broke out in Burlington, N. J. The physicians and city authorities did all in their power to check the dread disease and quiet the fears of the populace. One evening in September the Overseer of the Poor came into the Council chamber and reported that an old, lone shoemaker had died of the cholera in a lonely house in the suburbs, and that he, the overseer had made the necessary arrangements to bury him; had a grave dug in Potters' Field and everything ready, but he could not get any one to put the body in the coffin and bury it. The President, General Edward Burd Grubb, said: "The man must be buried; if I can get any one to help me I will do it. Meet me at midnight and show me where the body is. In the meantime, have a grave prepared in St. Mary's churchyard at my expense. I will not bury any one in Potters' Field." So, at midnight, General Grubb, with an old army friend (Bartlett, of Post No. 16), repaired to the lonely house, wrapped the corpse in blankets and put it in the wagon. General Grubb drove down to St. Mary's churchyard. After the body had been lowered into the grave General Grubb, remembering that he had been commissioned as a lay reader by the Bishop of New Jersey, for the purpose of administering the last rites of the church to any unfortunate soldier that might need his services during the war, went across the street to an old parishioner, borrowed a prayer-book and a candle, returned to the grave, and there, in the silent night, with uncovered head and reverential voice, he read the Episcopal service for the burial of the dead. And the poor, old, lone shoemaker, deserted by friends and neighbors, was laid to rest in consecrated ground. And over the grave one may still read on a stone placed there by General Grubb, "David Foster, died September, 1866."

> "And yet the world is full of men
> And women, too, who claim to be
> Possessed of courage to defend
> Their kind against adversity,
> But who have never learned the way
> To throw on others' paths a ray."

Success.

BY COMRADE COZZENS.

OUR canvassers have been telling many of our business citizens that "every man should advertise," said Comrade Cozzens. "I never knew any concern to make money without advertising."

"I have," said one of our citizens.

"What concern?"

"Why, the Philadelphia Mint. They make millions and never advertise."

A PIG was never known to wash, but a great many people have seen the pig iron.

"You have heard a cat pur, I suppose, George?"

"Yes, Mary, but outside of poetry you never heard a Cowper."

THE OLD ARMY HAVERSACK.

By Comrade Gilroy.

Last night I dreamed the shouts came back,
" What have you in your haversack?
I'm hungry, Comrade, as can be,
Have you some hard-tack left for me?
" It looks as though we boys at last
Must keep our forty days of fast!"
I wakened, and my thoughts went back,
To rummage through my haversack.

A weary march, a hopeless fight,
A sad retreat at dead of night,
And then we all at dawn of day
Lay down like cattle by the way ;
The pangs of hunger and of thirst
Were rending us like things accursed ;
A comrade shouted at my back,
" Come, open up your haversack."

Each spread his treasure at his feet,
In lieu of something there to eat :
A story-book, a testament,
A housewife by his mother sent,
And one a picture fair to see,
A baby on its mother's knee,
And so sweet scenes of home came back,
Around the empty haversack.

A comrade broke into a song
I was " Home, Sweet Home," and so a throng
Had gathered round us where we sat,
Of home and home delights to chat ;
Of tables laid with royal fare,
And served with woman's loving care
" Zip, zip" a volley swept our track
And each man grabbed his haversack.

A stricken comrade strove to rise,
The film of death was in his eyes,
" My haversack take there's some bread
A letter home," was all he said.
We caught him ere he sank to rest,
We crossed his hands above his breast,
His mother's picture, some hard-tack,
We found within his haversack

We broke the bread, and as I live,
It seemed the Lord was there to give,
The morsels were so magnified
By love of him who just had died ;
Whose spirit lingered round us there,
To solace us in our despair ;
And fling a ray of splendor back
To rest on memory's haversack.

O glad am I for dream that brings
So many half-forgotten things,
The Comradeship that closer grows
When sorrow darkest shadow throws ;
The comradeship that until death
Is breathed with every soldier's breath ;
That shares its crust in joy, or wrack,
From that old army haversack.

The Rich Irish Brogue.

By Comrade Dunn.

ALL dialects are amusing—the Irish, Scotch, Quaker, Yankee and Chinese. Each language has its brogue. A good instance of Irish brogue and blunder is instanced in Mrs. Kelly's cross-examination in the O'Toolihan suit for damages.

"You claim, Mrs. Kelly," said the Judge, "that Mrs. O'Toolihan gave you that bruised and blackened face ?"

"She did, yer Honor—indade she did, or I'm not born."

"And what you want is damages, Mrs. Kelly ?"

"It is damages, yez, says yer Honor? Damages ! No, bad luck ter the O'Toolihan. I have dam—ages enough. I wants sat-is-fac-shun, begorry !" (Laughter.)

Another case : John Quinn jerked his finger out of a box of turtles and held it up in great pain.

"What are you doing there, John ?" I asked.

Mosby Didn't Come.

By Comrade Henceman.

"SERGEANT, report without delay to the Adjutant for orders." "Very good, sir," was the prompt reply, and before many moments had passed the writer stood saluting before the Adjutant, at the same time repeating the usual routine sentence, "At your service, sir."

"Sergeant, reposing great confidence in your integrity, and believing you trustworthy in every respect, I detail you for special service. Report to these headquarters immediately after Retreat for instructions."

Such were the orders issued by the Adjutant of the 44th Infantry at White House Lot, Washington, D. C., during the impeachment of President Andrew Johnson.

Retreat sounded, roll was called and the writer forthwith reported at Headquarters and received instructions as follows, viz:

"Information has been received that an attack on the Treasury is contemplated by Mosby's men now organizing in Virginia, and that sympathizers are meeting nightly throughout the city."

"You will at once proceed to disguise yourself in citizen's clothing, and then visit all public halls and bar-rooms on the island, and report all suspicious gatherings coming under your observation. Be cautious, as much may depend upon your judgment and promptness."

In carrying out the order, the veteran of four years and three months' service in the field, was transformed to something very much like a dummy used before a second-hand clothing store, and in this role visited the island, searching high and low, walking to and fro, until the bell tolled off six o'clock A. M., finding no enemy; all quiet along the line. Returning to camp, I learned that special men were patrolling the grounds of the White House and War Department, guards were stationed at Cook's Bank, at Secretary Staunton's house, Record building, and in the basement of the War Department, as well as on all the doors of the building. Each man carried forty rounds of ammunition and had strict orders to halt every person within the limits of their post and to fire on all persons so refusing.

There was continual hurrying to and fro of officers in the War Department building, stopping only to exchange a few whispered instructions. The excitement reminded one of an evening before an engagement. This excitement and duties continuing for two weeks or longer.

Each day's awakening thought being that five hundred armed men would dash at midnight into the city, attack the Treasury and banking institutions, capture the moneys and effect their escape before we could offer resistance. An easy matter, too, as the heads of the nation were so involved that no available troops for immediate concentration could have been moved by an order from either the President, Secretary of War or the General of the Army, without a complication of authority, which, for the time being, would have caused riot and bloodshed within our own lines. To this day I feel like thanking Mosby for not capturing the boodle, and no doubt his many appointments to office by Grant were, in a measure, compensation for the big scare his name gave the Government.

Presence of Mind.

"THUS was I saved by mere presence of mind," said Pugsby, at the conclusion of a long story.

"Great thing—presence of mind. I might have been a rich man to-day if my presence of mind had not failed me at one time.

"Indeed? When was that?

"You remember my uncle George—rich old duffer. You know I am his heir. Well, sir, I was with him one day when he was taken with a fit. I was so frightened that I lost my presence of mind and called in a doctor, and uncle George is living yet."

-64-

Maj.-Gen. Geo. B. Mead.

THE HERO OF GETTYSBURG.

Sons of Veterans U. S. A.

I N the year 1881 Major A. P. Davis, of Pittsburg, Pa., conceived the idea that there should be an organization composed of the sons of those brave men who wore the blue in defence of their country and flag during those days from 1861 to 1865 which tried men's souls. Major Davis brought together a number of young men whose fathers served their country during the Civil War and formed a camp known as Davis Camp, No. 1, S. of V., U. S. A.

From that time we have continued to grow until now we have camps in every State and Territory in the Union. According to the last report from the Commander-in-Chief held at Paterson, N. J., September 10th, 11th, 12th, 13th and 14th, 1889, we have 1,770 camps, with a membership of 53,467 in good standing.

So, you see, we are growing, and will continue to do so, as we are able to recruit from day to day, like the order of the Cincinnatta ; we perpetuate by admitting our sons as soon as they become of age, so that Memorial Day and the memories of our fathers will never fade, but be kept green by us by placing on their mounds the choicest flowers of spring time.

We have among our membership some of the leading men of the country—sons of Grant, Sherman, Logan, Trenchard, Garfield, Clarkson, and last but not least, in our own city, the son of that invincible leader, Kearney.

This organization was opened unto us by our fathers' loyalty to their country and flag in time of war for freedom and equal rights to all men, so that we, their children, and our children might enjoy the blessings of a free home for all time under that spotless banner, the Red, White and Blue.

It is our duty as sons of those brave men to band ourselves together for the perpetuation of their memories and hand down to our children the same loyalty and love of country that our fathers have handed down to us by their hardships and privations on the battlefield and in the prison pen, laying bare their breasts to the enemy's shot and shell, that our flag might wave over us as a nation undivided, unsullied, and not a single star obscured. It is

66

our bonded duty to honor the veteran soldier, both living and dead, and this is what we are organized for. We should live up to our principles and objects as laid down to us as Sons of Veterans.

We should assist the veterans in caring for their sick and disabled comrades; also assist them on Memorial Day in strewing their departed comrades' graves with the choicest of flowers and the planting on their graves of the colors for which they fought and died.

The Grand Army of the Republic to-day is the largest and greatest organization in the world, but it has reached its zenith, and as year after year rolls on their ranks thin out, and ere long will have passed away, and it behooves us, the sons of those veterans, to be up and doing, so that when they are not left to attend to the decoration of their comrades' graves and the principles for which they fought, we, their sons, will be organized and ready to fill their places. Then let us go to work to build up our order and extend to the veteran soldier a cordial welcome to our meetings, so that they can see how we are working, and get their help and influence in building up our order.

> Soon the soldiers will be gathered
> To the fathers up above.
> Let us then be up and doing,
> Aiding in their work of love,
> Help them care for their old comrades
> Who are sick and in distress,
> 'Tis our duty thus to aid them,
> It is work that God will bless.

H. E. HATFIELD,
Post Col. Div. N. J. S. V. U. S. A.

Memories of Hancock.

BY THE COMMANDER OF PHIL SHERIDAN POST.

I MAY truly say that I am the only man in Newark who can claim thirty years of personal acquaintance with General Hancock, having been with him in the Seminole war of 1855, also in the Kansas trouble, and in the Utah war of 1858. In the Spring of 1858 I had the pleasure of being under him on the trip to Utah. At that time he was Captain Hancock, upon General Harney's staff, and was also Quartermaster. To write the history of that trip would fill a book. General Harney was ordered to march to Utah to take command in place of General Sidney Johnston, who was in command at that time; but General Harney never got there. It may have been for the best that he did not, but I am sure if he had we never would have had any more trouble with the Mormons. I believed then that General Harney knew from the start he would never reach Utah, for several times on the route we would encamp for one or two days at a time, waiting for orders from Washington. At one time we encamped at Fort Harney for nearly a week; then again at a place called the Cotton Woods, between Fort Harney and south crossing of the Platt river. Here he received orders to report at Washington, and from there he was sent to Washington Territory to settle the trouble between the English and American officers at that place. Almost everybody knows how that trouble turned out. General Scott had to be sent post-haste to settle the trouble between General Harney and the English officers, to prevent war.

Upon the return of General Harney from the Cotton Woods, Captain Hancock was ordered on to Oregon, with a lot of recruits at Fort Bridger. He left us and turned from the main road, and I did not see him again until I met him in the Army of the Potomac. Speaking of my personal knowledge of General Hancock's nature, I may say he was a very strict disciplinarian. He carried out all orders strictly to the letter himself, and made it a point to enforce it upon anyone under him, which made him the ideal and true soldier, and respected by every officer and private in his command. When he gave an order there were no questions to ask, because every officer or private knew he had to carry out that order to the letter, and I believe he never gave an order that he would not be willing to fill it himself in the same position. I have heard some complaint of his "tyranny," but old soldiers are hard to

Crescent  Sarsaparilla

✦ 100 DOSES--50 CENTS. ✦

✳ WHY YOU SHOULD TAKE IT ✳

1st.—Because we give you 100 doses for 50c.

2d.—Because we print on the label of the bottle the ingredients of Crescent Sarsaparilla, and you know just what you are taking. No secrecy as to ingredients.

3d. Because we guarantee to refund you your money if you obtain no benefit from taking Crescent Sarsaparilla.

4th.—Because the Crescent Drug Co., who prepare Crescent Sarsaparilla, are the largest Retail Druggists in the State of New Jersey, and are reliable, and stake the reputation and integrity of their retail business on the merits of Crescent Sarsaparilla.

5th.—Because we can and will mail you testimonials from our own city of absolute cures of Rheumatism, Gout, Kidney disease, Blood diseases, Skin diseases, etc., accomplished by Crescent Sarsaparilla. Send your name and address on a postal card to us and we will mail you testimonials.

☞ Why, therefore, will you continue to pay $1.00 or even 75c. for other makes of Sarsaparilla and secret made Patent Medicines, of which you know nothing, when you can purchase Crescent Sarsaparilla for 50c. a bottle and know just what you are taking, and have your money refunded if you are dissatisfied! Can anything be fairer than this?

⇢ MADE BY CRESCENT DRUG COMPANY, NEWARK, N. J. ↢

For · Sale · by · Druggists · Everywhere, · 50 · Cents · Per · Bottle.

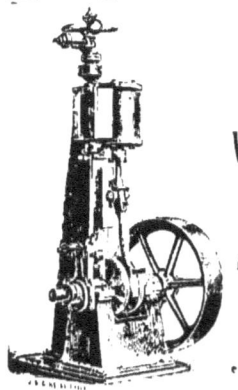

SEYMOUR & WHITLOCK,

43 LAWRENCE STREET,

Vertical Engines and Boilers

OF NEW DESIGN, FROM 3 TO 50 H. P.

We also furnish Exhaust and Circulating Fans,
Shafting, Hangers, Pulleys and General
Machinery.

⦁--- JOBBING PROMPTLY ATTENDED TO ⟿

FRANZ J. KASTNER'S

Phoenix Brewery

5 to 27 Lewis Street, - - Newark, N. J.

❄

◦——TELEPHONE No. 644——◦

Maj-Gen. Jos. Hooker,

OR FIGHTING JOE.

please. As the old saying is, some of the best soldiers are the greatest grumblers, and the fact is to grumble and complain is a soldier's comfort. Take that away from him and he is no good. Most of our old soldiers in the late war learned it then, and they have not got out of it to this day, and the most of them are getting too old to give it up now.

In a case of sickness or accident I always found General Hancock to be a kind-hearted and an affectionate man, always ready and willing to relieve distress. I well remember the time we were encamped at Fort Leavenworth fitting out the trains for Utah. He sent for me, and when I reported to him he said: "I want you to take great pains and examine every mule in the train, and every one that will not stand the trip to Utah turn it into the yard. Pick out the best mules, and nothing but the best, for you must know that we shall have to travel fast and long journeys." Some few days after I was ordered to have all the teams made fast to the wagons for inspection. Well, there was one very large bony mule that the officers did not think would stand the trip. Captain Hancock came to me and said : "Halleck, you had better turn that mule into the yard and get a better one." I said, "Captain, I will guarantee that mule will stand the trip." He said, "Well, you know that I do not want to discard any mules on the road." Several times he would ride up to me after we had traveled several hundreds of miles, and say, "Halleck, that mule is the best mule in the train." One day, when he was praising the mule, I said : "Captain, I don't know what I am going to do when we get to the mountains." "Why?" says he. "Because the tongue of the wagon is not long enough for that mule. The hair upon his tail is all worn off now." "Get a longer tongue," says he. "Captain," I said, "I have measured every wagon tongue in the train, and this is the longest one I can find." "Well," says he, "keep the head, legs and body ; never mind the tail part."

Keeping One's Eyes Open.

BY COMRADE JAS. COLLER.

COMRADES. To get through this world a man must look about him and even sleep with one eye open; for there are many baits for fishes, many nets for birds, and many traps for men. While foxes are so common, we must not be geese. There is a very great difference in this matter among people of my acquaintance; many see more with one eye than others with two, and many have fine eyes and cannot see a jot. All heads are not sense-boxes. Some are so cunning that they suspect everybody, and so live all their lives in miserable fear of their neighbors; others are so simple that every knave takes them in. One man tries to see through a brick wall, and hurts his eyes; while another finds a hole in it, and sees as far as he pleases. Some work at the mouth of a furnace and are never scorched, and others burn their hands at the fire when they only mean to warm them. Now, it is true that no one can give another experience, and we must all pick up wit for ourselves; yet I shall venture to give some of the homely cautions which have served my turn, and perhaps they may be of use to others, as they have been to me.

Nobody is more like an honest man than a thorough rogue. When you see a man with a great deal of religion displayed in his shop window you may depend upon it he keeps a very small stock of it within. Do not choose your friend by his looks; handsome shoes often pinch the feet. Don't be fond of compliments; remember, "Thank you, pussy, and thank you, pussy," killed the cat. Don't believe in the man who talks most, for mewing cats are very seldom good mousers. By no means put yourself in another person's power; if you put your thumb between two grinders, they are very apt to bite. Drink nothing without seeing it; sign nothing without reading it, and make sure that it means no more than it says. Don't go to law unless you have nothing to lose; lawyer's houses are built on fools' heads. In any business, never wade into water where you cannot see the bottom. Put no dependence upon a label of a bag, and count money after your own ken. See the sack opened before you buy what is in it; for he who trades in the dark asks to be cheated. Keep clear of the man who does not value his own character. Beware of everyone who swears; he who would blaspheme his Maker would make no bones of lying or stealing. Beware of no man more than of yourself: we carry our worst enemies within us. When a new opinion or doctrine comes up before you, do not bite till you know whether it is bread or a stone; and do not be sure that the gingerbread is good because of the gilt on it. Never shout hello! till you are quite out of the woods; and don't cry fried fish till they are caught in the net.

Be shy of people who are over-polite, and don't be too fast with those who are forward and rough. When you suspect a design in anything, be on your guard; set the trap as soon as you smell a rat, but mind you don't catch your own fingers in it. Have very little to do with a boaster, for his beer is all froth; and, though he brags that all his goods and even his copper kettles are gold and silver, you will soon find out that a boaster and a liar are first cousins. Commit all your secrets to no man; trust in God with all your heart, but let your confidence in friends be weighed in balances of prudence, seeing that men are but men, and all men are frail. Trust not great weights to slender threads; yet be not ever-more suspicious for suspicion is a cowardly virtue at best. Men are not angels—remember that; but they are not devils, and it is too bad to think them so.

List of Prizes and Donations.

One Pair Fancy Slippers, Geo. B. Clark.

One Illustrated History of Bible Animals, P. F. Mulligan.

One Fancy Picture and Ornamental Mat, Theodore B. Munn.

One Gas Stove and Broiler, The Stewart Manufacturing Co.

Parlor Suit, Phil. Sheridan Post.

One Ornamental Oak Stand, Chas. Cannon.

One Extension Table, A. Kuhner

Steel Engraving of Gen. Grant, Phil. Sheridan Post.

Foster's History of New Jersey and the Rebellion, Francis J. Meeker.

One Pair Mantel Vases, Union Pacific Tea Co.

One Quarter's (3 months) Tuition, from date of entry, to Newark Business College, Phil. Sheridan Post.

Selection of Wall Paper, value $5, Phil. Sheridan Post.

One Year's Subscription to Sunday Standard, F. M. McDermit & Co.

One Pair Large Mantel Vases, Sarah Daley.

One Oxidized Silver Manicure Set, Frank H. McCully.

One Boy's Printing Press, Thomas Bowles.

Cash Gift, $5, James A. Cove & Co.

Cash Gift, $5, James Johnson.

Cash Gift, $1, Arthur W. Palmer.

Cash Gift, $1, Irvington Smelting Works, Glorieux & Woolsey.

One Fruit Dish (fancy glass), Phil. Sheridan Post.

One Oil Painting, Frank Long.

One Banquet Lamp, W. T. Mersereau & Co.

One Pair Suspenders, Jacob Herman.

One Electric Bell and Appliances Complete, Alfred Sommer.

Two Bottles (large cut glass) Extra Fine Cologne, C. B. Smith.

One Work Box, A. Patterson.

One Quart Bottle Writing Fluid, Pomroy & Sons.

One Pot Plant, Begerow & Gerlack.

Two Pairs Carving Knives and Forks, Macknet & Doremus.

One Picture (Love of Country), Phil. Sheridan Post.

One Pot plant, Chas. Witheridge.

One Pair Corsets, Aaron Gries & Bros.

One Fancy Match Safe, Clara Schaler.
One Barrel of Potatoes, J. W. Fisher.
One Barrel of Potatoes, F. E. Kelsey.
One Cigar Stand, John Schuldnecht.
One Cup and saucer, Mrs. Ida Schuldnecht.
One Glass Pitcher, Mrs. Mary Garabrant.
One Butter Dish, Mrs. G. Garabrant.
One Pickle Dish, Mrs. G. Garabrant.
One Gold Gilded Vase Jug, Mrs. Batterson.
One Gold Gilded Vase Bottle, A Friend of the Post.
One Pair Vases, Mrs. W. Healy.
One Vase, Mrs. Annie Walters.
Two Sacks of Flour, Wolf & Weber.
One Barrel of Potatoes, Aaron M. Garabrant.
One Box of Cigars, G. Hauck.
One Pair of Fine Woollen Blankets, Heath & Drake.
One Eight-Day Clock, Jean Tack.
One Gold Pen and Pen Holder, H. Ginger.
One Silver Spoon Holder, James Traphagan.
One Linen Table Cover, Davis & Co.
One-quarter Dozen Ladies' Toilet, Seidler & Co.
One Woollen Ulster, L. Frauhauf.
One Wax Doll, Hines & Son.
One Umbrella, Ed. F. Fielder.
One Case (12 boxes) K. K. K., F. E. Crane & Co.
One Pair Gents' Shoes, William Wengel.
One Extra Fine Clothes Brush, E. & W. Dixon.
Two Fuel Cartridges, Gardner & Watson.
One G. A. R. Hat, Complete, Corrigan (The Hatter).
One Nickle Alarm Clock, Richard Smith & Co.
One Boys' Metal Wheelbarrow, Phil. Sheridan Post.
Two Large Cans Baking Powder, Mrs. Yeager.
One Box of Cigars, Dr. Iliff.
One Oil Painting, John Walsh.
Two Boxes of Cigars, Chas. W. Mink.
One Spring Bed, M. J. O'Connor.
One Hand Satchel, T. P Peddie & Co.
One Bed-room Set (Complete), Phil. Sheridan Post.
One Dinner Set of 150 Pieces, Phil. Sheridan Post.
One Pair of Fancy Slippers, A. Hood.
One Ham, Charles Weigand.
One Ebony Gavel, John Cohaut.
One Banjo, Frank Blass.
One Kalsomine Brush, Wm. Murray & Co.

One Oil Painting, 24x36, James Van Horn.
One Oil Painting, Fred. Buck.
One Cake Dish, Anna Stansberry.
One Fruit Dish, Hahn & Co
One Pair Vases, William Weed.
One Hat, Mr. Fairchild.
One Pair Pants, Mr. Fisher.
One Box of Candy, French Mixture, A. C. Navatier.
Four Pictures (The Seasons), Chemical Works Chas. Cooper & Co.
Two Boxes of Toilet Soap, F. V. Rodeman.
One Hat, J. F. Ehler (The Hatter).
One Box of Cigars, E. P. Hassinger.
One Box of Cigars, N. P. Marsh.
One Pair (Alligator) Slippers, Marks Born-Stein.
Two Hand Satchels, Wm. Hedley Sons.
One Silk Hat, Tunison, Lewis & Co.
One Set Ideal Irons, Bless & Drake.
One Pair Fancy Slippers, J. Coppersmith.
One Bag of Flour, Alderman Young.
One Plated French Coffee Pot, Wm. H. Drummond.
One Pair of Boots, John Shearen.
One Pair of Shoes, John Shearen.
One Parlor Lamp, Schwartzwalder.
One Spring Lamb, F. McGuinness.
One Pair of Imported Japan Pictures, David Nathan.
Two Boxes of Cigars, Geo. Grimm.
One Ham, S. Fishel.
One Pair of Shoes, G. Heidman.
One Ham, Fred. Hahn.
One Fancy Ornamental Lamp Shade, Miss Mannie Johnson.
One Turkey Rug, Miss Amelia L. Peters.
One Set of Vases, Jennie Hallock.
One Large Lamp, Fannie Hallock.
One Large Lamp, Mrs. Sternkopp.
One Box of Cigars, J. Mendel.
One Rule, Belcher Bros.
One Rule, S. O. Smith
One Axe, C. A. De Hard & Son.
One Pair of Slippers, Chas. Horton.
One Pair of Dress Pants to Order, M. Marbe & Son.
One Plush Album, McManus Bros.
One Sack of Flour, Geo. Miller.
One Bottle of Cognac Brandy, Jacob Pfohl.
One Pair of Shoe Uppers, Munden & Rummel.
One Box of Cigars, Chas. Smith.

LIST OF PRIZES.--Continued.

One Box of Cigars, D. J. Eming.
Two Sacks of Flour, Cort Bros.
Two Sacks of Flour, R. L. Chambers & Co.
Five Bottles of Wine, Andrew Volk.
One Ladies' Hand Satchell, Alderman McCormac.
One Fancy French Clock and Glass Case, Phil. Sheridan Post.
One Silver Castor, Phil. Sheridan Post.
Cash Gift, $5, G. A. L.
Cash Gift, $5, G. A. Halsey.
Cash Gift, $5, Gotfried Kreuger.
Cash Gift, $10, Joseph Hensler.
Cash Gift, $1, Marshall & Ball.
Cash Gift, $5, John L. Armitage.
Cash Gift, $2, C. N. Lockwood.
Cash Gift, $5, J. F. Connolly.
Cash Gift, $5, Marcus S. Richards.
Cash Gift, $3, F. Weibke.
Cash Gift, $2, F. Luthry.
Cash Gift, 50 cents, H. Burner.
Cash Gift, 50 cents, Chas. Mayer.
Cash Gift, 50 cents, Adam Turkes.
Cash Gift, $2, F. J. Castner.
Cash Gift, $3, Wm. Hill.
Cash Gift, $2, From a Friend.
Cash Gift, $11, from Friends through Comrade Soden.
Cash Gift, 50 cents, J. Hudson.
Cash Gift, $1, Clara Dykman.
Cash Gift, $1, Conant & Sons.
Cash Gift, $1, Mr. Reuben Trier.
Cash Gift, $2.50, from Friends, through J. W. Jones.
Cash Gift, $1, From a Friend.
Cash Gift, $10, from Friends, through Fred. Buck.
Cash Gift, $1.50, John Shearon.
One-half Ton of Coal (order), Alderman P. Ulrich.
Cash Gift, $1.75, from Friends, through Mary Garabrant.
One Suit of Men's Clothing, Colyer & Co.
One Tambourine, G. Shepley.
One Box Cigars, Mr. McCluskey.
One Whisk Broom and Case (with Mirror), Mrs. Laura Peters.
One Pair Calfskin Shoes (order), John E. Albert.
Cash Gift, $3, E. B. Woodruff.
One Gallon Wine (in four bottles), P. X. Devivaux.
One Fancy Knitted Tidy, Miss Lillie Remington.

Cash Gift, $10, E. G, B.
One Chamber Toilet Set, Mrs. Mary Hallock.
One Bag Flour, Mr. Dennison.
One Painting, Country Scene, R. Loepsinger.
One Artistic Picture, Frederick Keers' Sons.
One Box Tea (5 lbs.), M. Fagan.
One Large Wedding Cake, H. L. Hallock.
One Bottle of Bay Rum, A. Koellhoffer.
Five Bottles Wine, Richard Verrinno.
One Pair Child's Slippers, Lowey Bros.
One Lamp, Stein & Blau.
One Crazy Quilt, Mrs. Walters.
One Cake Dish, Miss Annie Farrington.
Cash Gift, 50 cents, Mathew Crooks.
Twenty-eight Pictures of General Grant (steel plate), Phil Sheridan Post.
One Box French Candy, Charles Winkler.
One Load of Wood (delivered), David Ripley & Sons.
One Suit Men's Clothes, Marshall & Ball.
One Box Toilet Soap (100 cakes), C. W. Rothe.
Cash Gift, $5, Hon. Geo. J. Ferry.
One Pair Driving Gloves, William P. Ward.
One Axe, M. Price.
One Suit Child's Clothing, Stoutenberg & Co.
One Lambrequin, David Straus.
Four Whips, Phil Sheridan Post.
One Child's Rocker, Campbell & Kean.
One Comrade's Cap (Shaving Kit), Wm. A. Baker.
One Hat, A Friend of the Post.
One Desk Rule, S. O. Smith.
One Glass Panel (decorated), C. Belcher.
One Box Novelties, &c., E. Huebner & Sons.
Cash Gift, $4.25, Mrs. Dallas, through friends.
One Violin Bow, Joseph Thome.
One Violin, Phil Sheridan Post.
One Can (25 lbs.), Yellow Ocre, A. C. Getchers.
One Box Borax Soap, H. Hunkele.
Twenty-four Velvet Work-Boxes, Geo. A. Clark & Brother.
One Pair Vases, Cash Gift, 25 cents, Mrs. Riker.
Cash Gift, 25 cents, J. S. Morris.
One Pitcher, One Pickle Dish, Miss Mary E. Mahah.
One Half Ton Coal (order), Delaware & Hudson Canal Co.
Shaving Cup and Brush, F. P. Fleming.
One Set Silver-Plated Tea Spoons, Phil Sheridan Post.
One Silver Butter Dish, Phil Sheridan Post.
One Silver Butter Dish, Phil Sheridan Post.
One Singer Machine, Phil Sheridan Post.

One and a Half Dozen Boxes Ginger Snaps, Hetfield & Ducker.

One Hat (to order), James Moon.

One Dozen Snowflake Flour Packages, Jacob Gulick.

One Dozen Superlative Flour Packages, James Marlatt.

One Overcoat, McGregor & Co.

One Ottoman, C. Osborne.

One Handsomely Chased Silver Ice Pitcher, R. Gray.

One Pair Roller Skates, P. Loewentraut.

One Gold Watch Chain, Henry Aurinhammer.

One Umbrella, Francis Devlin.

One Fancy Japanese Cane, Captain Michael Corbett.

One Box Cigars, Miles F. Quinn.

One Box Cigars, Wm. P. Stapleton.

One Eight-Day Clock, Phil Sheridan Post.

One Pair Vases, Union Pacific Tea Co.

One Gallon Whiskey, Samuel Maddy.

Cash Gifts, $2.50, From Friends, through Comrade Buck.

One Canary Bird, W. England.

One Bottle Brandy, Mr. Demerman.

One Meerschaum Smoking Set, Robt. G. Gerth.

One Box Assorted Confectionery, Gerdes.

Two Ladies' Breast Pins (gold), Fredk. Byron.

One Ottoman Foot Rest, Riley & Osborne.

One Silver Card Basket, Phil Sheridan Post.

Twelve Bars Soap, Mrs. Huniel.

One Pickle and Preserve Dish, Geo. Garabrant.

One Box Tea, M. Fagan.

One Pair Extra Good Suspenders, Wm. J. Douglass.

One Box Cigars, Richard Garabrant.

One Ink Stand, Mrs. Joseph Colyer.

One Lamp (complete), Neal Scow & Co.

Glass Set (3 pieces), H. Keller.

Two Pounds Coffee, R. G. Schaff.

One Pair Slippers, Geo. B. Clark.

One Pair Pants (made to order), Geo. W. Morningstern.

Glass Set (4 pieces), Miss Ella Garabrant.

One Pair Slippers, Taylor & Williams.

One Child's Kilt Suit, J. A. Lutz.

One Whisk Broom and Holder, Mr. Gaddis.

One Barrel Potatoes, C. Walters & Co.

One Knife (pocket), Jeff. Cort.

One Pocket Knife, Mr. Eckert.

One Hat (order), Geo. Rommel.

One-half ton of Coal, F. Feyen, Jr.

One Lamp, Wm. Stainsby.

One Card Basket, (silver) B. J. Mayo.

All Gifts for Prizes or Donations not mentioned in this book, will be acknowledged through the public press.

Maj.-Gen. H. Judson Kilpatrick.

WHY WE WEAR THE BADGE; OR, THE VETERAN AND HIS GRANDSON.

BY COMRADE JACK CRAWFORD.

Hold on! Hold on! My goodness, you take my breath, my son,
A-firin' questions at me, like shots from a Gatlin' gun
Why do I wear this eagle an' flag an' brazen star,
An' why do my old eyes glisten when somebody mentions war?
An' why do I call men "comrade," an' why do my eyes grow bright,
When you hear me tell your grandma I'm going to Post to-night?
Come here, you inquisitive rascal, and set on your grandpa's knee,
An' I'll try an' answer the broadsides you've been a-firin' at me.

Away back there in the sixties, and long afore you were born,
The news come a-flashing to us, one bright an' sunny morn,
That some of our Southern brothers, a-thinkin', no doubt, 'twar right,
Had trailed their guns on our banner, an' opened a nasty fight.
The great big guns war a-boomin', an' the shot flying thick an' fast,
An' troops all over the southland war rapidly bein' massed,
An' a thrill went through the nation, a fear that our glorious land
Might be split an' divided an' ruined by mistaken brothers' hand.

Lord! but wa'nt there excitement, an' didn't the boys' eyes flash?
An' didn't we curse our brothers fur bein' so foolish an' rash?
An' didn't we raise the neighbors with loud and continued cheers,
When Abe sent out a dockyment a-callin' for volunteers?
An' didn't we flock to the colors when the drums began to beat?
An' didn't we march with proud step along this village street?
An' didn't the people cheer us when we got aboard the cars,
With the flag a-wavin' o'er us, and went away to the wars?

I'll never forgit your grandma as she stood outside o' the train,
Her face as white as the snowdrift, her tears a-fallin' like rain
She stood there quiet and death-like, 'mid all o' the rush an' noise,
Fur the war war a-takin' from her her husband an' three brave boys
Bill, Charlie and little Tommy—just turned eighteen, but as true
An' gal ant a little soldier as ever wore the blue.
It seemed almost like murder for to tear her poor heart so,
But your grandad *couldn't* stay, baby, an' the boys war determined to go.

The evenin' afore we started she called the boys to her side,
An' told 'em as how they war always their mother's joy an' pride,
An' though her soul was in torture, an' her poor heart bleedin' an' sore
An' though she needed her darlings, their country needed 'em more.
She told 'em to do their duty wherever their feet might roam,
An' to never forgit in battle their mother war prayin' at home,
An' if (an' the tears nigh chocked her) they should fall in front o' the foe,
She'd go to her Blessed Saviour and ax Him to lighten the blow,

Bill lays an' awaits the summons 'neath Spottsylvania's sod,
An' on the field of Antietam Charley's spirit went back to God;
An' Tommy, our baby Tommy, we buried one starlit night
Along with his fallen comrades, just after the Wilderness fight.
The lightnin' struck our family tree, an' stri iped it off every limb,
A-leavin' only this bare old trunk, a-standin' alone an' grim.
My boy, that's why your grandma, when you kneel to the God you love,
Makes you ax Him to watch your uncles, an' make 'em happy above.

That's why you sometimes see her with tear-drops in her eyes;
That's why you sometimes catch her a-trying to hide her sighs;
That's why, at our great reunions, she looks so solemn and sad;
That's why her heart seems a-breakin' when the boys are so jolly an' glad;
That's why you sometimes find her in the bedroom overhead,
Down on her knees a-prayin', with their pictures laid out on the bed.
That's why the old-time brightness will light up her face no more,
Till she meets her hero warriors in the camp on the other shore.

An' when the great war was over, back came the veterans true,
With not one star a-missin' from the azure field of blue;
An' the boys who on field o' battle had stood the fiery test
Formed Posts o' the great Grand Army in the North, South, East an' the West.
Fraternity, Charity, Loyalty, is the motto 'neath which they train—
Their objects to care for the helpless, an' banish sorrow an' pain
From the homes o' the widows an' orphans of the boys who have gone before,
To answer their names at roll call in that great Grand Army Corps.

An' that's why we wear these badges, the eagle an' flag an' star,
Worn only by veteran heroes who fought in that bloody war;
An' that's why my old eyes glisten while talkin' about the fray,
An' that's why I call men "comrade" when I meet 'em every day;
An' that's why I tell your grandma "I'm going to Post to-night."
For there's where I meet the old boys who stood with me in the fight,
An', my child, that's why I've taught you to love and revere the men
Who come here a-wearin' badges to fight those battles again.

They are the gallant heroes who stood 'mid the shot an' shell,
An' follered the flyin' colors right into the mouth o' hell—
They are the men whose valor saved the land from disgrace and shame,
An' lifted her back in triumph to her perch on the dome of fame;
An' as long as you live, my darling, till your pale lips in death are mute,
When you see that badge on a bosom, take off your hat an' salute;
An' if any ol' vet. should halt you an' question why you do,
Just tell him you've got a right to, fur your grandad's a comrade, too.

AT THE FIRESIDE.

At nightfall by the firelight's cheer,
My little Margaret sits me near,
And begs me tell of things that were
When I was little just like her.

Ah, little lips you touch the spring
Of sweetest sad remembering,
And hearth and heart flash all aglow
With ruddy tints of long ago.

I at my father's fireside sit,
Youngest of all who circle it,
And beg him tell me what did he
When he was little just like me.

                        John D. Long

AMERICA.

My country! 'tis of thee,
Sweet land of liberty,
  Of thee I sing:
Land where my fathers died!
Land of the pilgrims' pride!
From every mountain side
  Let freedom ring'

My native country, thee,
Land of the noble, free,
  Thy name I love;
I love thy rocks and rills,
My heart with rapture thrills
  Like that above.

Let music swell the breeze,
And ring from all the trees
  Sweet freedom's song:
Let mortal tongues awake;
Let all that breathe partake;
Let rock their silence break,
  The sound prolong.

Our fathers' God ! to thee,
Author of liberty,
  To thee we sing :
Long may our land be bright
With freedom's holy light;
Protect us by thy might,
  Great God, our King!

www.ingramcontent.com/pod-product-compliance
Lightning Source LLC
Chambersburg PA
CBHW032355020726

47499CB00008B/2765